Faith and Trust

Faith and Trust

Blake Karrington

www.urbanbooks.net

Urban Books, LLC
300 Farmingdale Road, NY-Route 109
Farmingdale, NY 11735

ISBN 13: 978-1-64556-202-3
ISBN 10: 1-64556-202-6

First Trade Paperback Printing May 2021
Printed in the United States of America

10 9 8 7 6 5 4 3 2 1

This is a work of fiction. Any references or similarities to actual events, real people, living or dead, or to real locales are intended to give the novel a sense of reality. Any similarity in other names, characters, places, and incidents is entirely coincidental.

Distributed by Kensington Publishing Corp.
Submit Orders to:
Customer Service
400 Hahn Road
Westminster, MD 21157-4627
Phone: 1-800-733-3000
Fax: 1-800-659-2436

Faith and Trust

by

Blake Karrington

Chapter One

Faith was awakened by her boyfriend Trust's hard dick poking into her backside. She eyed the clock on the cable box while licking her lips. She had the day off, but she knew that Trust was usually up and preparing for his day around 9:00 a.m. It was only 8:00, which meant they had time to have some fun.

Faith backed into Trust and bounced her ass slightly as she did so. When that didn't wake him, she decided to stop being subtle. Reaching behind her, she placed her hand inside his boxer briefs and began to jack him off slowly. A sneaky grin spread across her face as Trust stirred. Just the thought of him being inside of her made Faith moist, and since Trust was already hard, foreplay wasn't needed. Faith slept naked, so all she had to do was sit up and gently push Trust onto his back. Just as he was opening his eyes, she was straddling him, and the head of his penis was inches away from her opening. Grinning at her man, Faith slid down onto his dick, causing him to let out a deep moan.

Faith bit her bottom lip as she began to move up and down, staring Trust in the eyes as she did so. His hands gripped her waist, and his gaze penetrated her soul. One of Faith's hands cupped her breast, while the other softly gripped a mass of Trust's jet-black curls. He used his hands to guide her ass up and down his shaft. His dick was long enough to reach her G-spot on its own, but the friction that her clit was receiving from being on top of him was overwhelming. Faith pinched her nipple and let out a shrill yelp as waves of pleasure rolled through her body during an intense orgasm. That was all the motivation Trust needed. He flipped Faith onto her back and began to drill into her middle as she clawed at his back.

"I love you," Faith whispered in his ear as she wrapped her arms around his body, clinging to him like she never wanted to let go.

With the deep penetration of Trust's dick filling her love tunnel, she could feel the tip of his dick hitting the back of her wall with every stroke. Her body jumped every time his dick touched her bottom. His thickness rubbed across her G-spot, causing her to have multiple orgasms back-to-back. The combination of her wetness and the tightening of her muscles pleased Trust as much as it pleased her. When he couldn't take it anymore, Trust gritted his teeth as his seeds spilled into Faith.

Breathless, he slid out of her while she curled into a fetal position and began to suck her thumb. Trust chuckled at her. "Nah, ma. You woke me up, and now you want to go back to sleep? You aren't going to cook your man breakfast?" he asked as he headed for the master bathroom to take a shower.

"Of course I am. Just let me lie here for five minutes." She closed her eyes as Trust once again laughed. With a smile on her face, Faith lay on silk sheets and tried to recover from the lovemaking she had just experienced. After two years with Trust, their sex life was still amazing.

Managing to catch herself before she dozed off, Faith got out of bed and grabbed her gray silk robe from the closet. She had all day to chill. If her man wanted breakfast, that was what he would get. Faith wasn't exactly sure just what Trust did all day when he was at work. He owned a convenience store in the hood, but he didn't actually work in the store. He had someone to do that for him.

He also had some rental properties he rented out to Section 8. So even though he had a few different streams of income, he didn't necessarily have an office to go to every day. All Faith really knew was that he took very good care of her. The newly built condo they lived in cost a pretty penny to rent each month, and when Trust wasn't spoiling her with bags and shoes, they were going on lavish trips. Faith saw no need to question him about his day-to-day activities. The bills got paid, and that was all she felt she needed to know.

Trust entered the kitchen just as she was scooping a hefty serving of scrambled eggs onto his plate. "What you got planned for today?" he asked, smacking her on the ass.

Trust stood six feet four inches while Faith only stood five feet four inches. He was muscular with dark skin, and she had a curvy body that resembled the one that Kim Kardashian paid for. Shit, Faith's was better, because her thighs were proportionate to her ass. She'd heard many times over the years that she resembled actress Lauren London. A major difference, however, was that instead of the long tresses most women rocked, Faith opted for super-short cuts most times. She only wore long weaves every now and then.

"Barbie, Elaine, and I are going to lunch. That's all I have planned for today."

Trust frowned up his face at the mention of Barbie. He hated her stuck-up ass, and he hated her parents for naming her Barbie. Faith knew he hated her best friend, so there was no need to elaborate.

"Word? I'll probably be in a little earlier than usual tonight. Maybe around eight."

Faith smiled at the news. Most nights, Trust didn't make it in before eleven, and since she worked at the hospital, most nights Faith was in bed by ten. She hated when he would come in late and wake her up for sex. Then they'd be up into the wee hours of the morning, and she'd be tired as hell at work. She wished he worked regular nine-to-five hours instead of dope-boy hours. Still, she kept the complaining to a minimum.

Trust wasted no time scarfing down his breakfast, and then he pecked Faith on the lips and headed out to his black ZX-11 motorcycle. Trust only drove his motorcycle on special occasions, and today was a special occasion. He pulled his helmet onto his head and hopped on his bike, heading to meet his homies Zoe and Gutta.

"Everybody get ya fucking hands in the air now! Now goddamn it!" Trust screamed as he burst through the front doors of the bank. "If you move or say anything without being asked, I'ma shoot the motherfucker standing next to you for your lack of cooperation. This will all be over in a few seconds, folks. This is not your money. Don't die trying to protect it," he warned the frightened patrons of the bank he and his crew had just barged into.

His partner Gutta jumped onto the counter with one vertical leap, pointing the 9 mm he was gripping in his gloved hands at the tellers, while demanding that they back away from their registers. Zoe stood at the front door ready to encounter anybody who walked through. Trust began to handle the customers and the employees who were now laid out on the floor terrified.

"Sixty seconds!" Trust yelled out to Gutta after glancing at his wrist. Gutta had begun to empty out the registers, separating the dye packs from the money in the process. "Let's move! Let's move!" he shouted, getting Gutta to move on to the vault. "Forty-five seconds!"

Gutta cleaned out the teller registers and looked around to find the manager sitting on the floor among a group of customers. Gutta grabbed a fistful of his hair, lifting the man to his feet. The manager was scared as fuck, looking at the masked gunmen in front of him.

"Open the fucking vault," Gutta demanded, jamming his gun into the gut of the manager. "I'm only gonna ask you once."

The manager complied without thinking twice, opening the vault with a key that was attached to an elastic band he had wrapped around his wrist. His hands were shaking so frantically he could barely stick the key in the hole. He had never looked down the barrel of a gun, especially not one possessed by a man who had a look in his eyes as though he wouldn't hesitate to pull the trigger. The eyes the bank manager stared into were cold and emotionless. Pure evil.

"Now sit yo' ass down," Gutta said, pushing the manger back to the floor once the door was open.

"Thirty seconds!" Trust yelled out from the floor. "Let's go! Let's go!" he yelled.

Gutta got into the vault and went straight to work filling the small duffle bag with the money lying out on the shelves. He even took a bag after he looked into it and saw all silver coins inside. After pretty much cleaning out the vault, Gutta looked over and saw a small safe on the floor in the corner by itself.

"Fifteen seconds!" Trust yelled out. "We gotta go! We gotta go!" he yelled out to Gutta urgently.

With his mind set on the small safe, Gutta ran over and grabbed the manager off the floor and pulled him over to the safe by his hair. He knew that he didn't have much time, but he had to try his hand.

"Open it," Gutta demanded, pressing the gun against his head.

"I can't," the manager whimpered, closing his eyes. "This safe is on a timer, and if I try to open it, the alarm

will go off. It's not set to open until two this afternoon,"
he explained.

"We gotta go! We gotta go!" Trust yelled, running into
the vault, cutting Gutta's conversation short.

He wanted to hit the safe bad, but he knew his time
was up. Trust and Gutta stormed out of the vault and
demanded that all the customers and employees get into
the vault. Once the last head made it into the vault, the
three men left the bank. Outside were three motorcycles.
Along with Trust's black ZX-11 were Gutta's green Suzuki
R6 and Zoe's green one. He had a bike just like Gutta.
Back-to-back they all sped off and headed down the highway trying to get as far away from the bank as possible.
The robbery took a little more than sixty seconds, and it
was done on a professional level, leaving behind little to
no evidence at all.

No one knew, not even the women in their lives, that
Trust, Gutta, and Zoe were skilled bank robbers known
as the Bank Boyz.

Chapter Two

"Don't you look pretty," Barbie stated with a smile as she stood up to greet Faith. The two were meeting in an upscale Italian restaurant, one of Faith's favorites.

She often had to wonder if Trust was right when he said that Barbie wasn't really her friend. Friends accept you for who you are, and they lift you up instead of tearing you down. Barbie had no problem lifting up anyone who was up to her standards. Before lunch, Faith changed her outfit twice just so she would meet Barbie's approval, and even she had to admit that was a little ridiculous. But the woman wasn't all bad. She and Barbie had been friends since high school, and they had quite a few good times.

"Thank you," Faith stated, pleased that Barbie approved of the yellow wrap dress she'd chosen to wear. "Are we waiting for Elaine?" Faith inquired as the hostess approached.

Barbie waved her off. "She's always late, and I'm ready for a glass of wine at least. The hostess can show her to our table when she gets here."

Whenever they all linked up, or even when it was just Faith and Barbie, Barbie was always expected to make decisions. As the daughter of a judge and a teacher, Barbie was naturally bossy and a take-charge kind of person. Her older sister, Angela, was an FBI agent, and Barbie was the spoiled brat of the family. Her career in interior design wasn't as prominent as her parents' or her sister's, but it funded her lifestyle. That and her boy-friend, Clinton, who was the branch manager of a bank.

"So, tell me more about this trip to Dubai," Barbie said with a grin after the women were seated. She placed her very expensive Birkin bag on the empty seat next to her.

Faith's eyes lit up at the mention of her trip. "Oh, my gosh, I'm so excited. In three weeks, Trust and I will be spending five days in Dubai. I can't wait. I have so much vacation time that I'm taking two weeks off. This will be a much-needed vacation. And my period will be done by that time, so there's no limit to the nasty shit that can be done in that gorgeous hotel suite." Faith got horny just thinking about it.

Barbie raised her eyebrows curiously. "And your man only owns one convenience store in the hood? Those rental properties must bring in a pretty penny, because I can't see the money from the store paying the rent on that condo. Don't tell me Trust has you over there footing the bills," Barbie said, prying for information.

Barbie's man made good money, but he wasn't rich by far. The fact that he had excellent credit and many credit cards were among the main reasons he could get Barbie nice things. Once they moved in together, he paid all the bills while she used her money from work-ing to pretty much spoil herself. So even though her man paid the bills and did nice things for her here and there, all her designer shit came from her own money. Barbie wanted to know how it was that Trust could pro-vide Faith with a better lifestyle than her man, who made more than $50,000 a year, provided her. Surely, Trust wasn't making more than that from one rinky-dink store and a few rental properties. The two-bedroom condo in the Northeast section of Philadelphia cost far more than the income he would make selling sodas, chips, and sandwiches. Faith knew that as well, but the love she had for him wouldn't allow her to question him about anything he told her, even though in the back of her mind she felt he might have been selling drugs from the way he spent large amounts of money on her.

Faith shifted uncomfortably in her seat, wondering why Barbie was watching her man's pockets. "I can assure you that Trust doesn't ask me for one dime of my money. I don't even have to buy groceries," Faith snidely replied. She was offended, and she wasn't trying to hide it.

Barbie held her hands up in surrender. Offending a person wasn't quite enough to make her stop prying or throwing shade. "Hey, I'm just saying. It's not really adding up. He does look a little thuggish. You sure he's not selling drugs or something? You know you always had a thing for the rough types." Barbie grinned as Faith rolled her eyes in disgust.

No one knew that the few times Barbie saw Trust, she was instantly aroused. The tone of his voice and the bulge of his muscles made her pussy throb. She was low-key infatuated with the thuggish type, but she would never lower her standards enough to deal with a man who did illegal shit. Not coming from the family she came from.

"Let's stop talking about my man." Faith snatched the menu up with an attitude, causing Barbie to giggle.

Faith had never been one to question the things Trust told her. She just trusted and believed everything he said, but she was starting to wonder if that made her foolish.

After the robbery, Trust, Gutta, and Zoe met up at their hideout deep in the heart of Southwest Philly. Trust had bought the house after their second robbery just so they could have a place to chill and count money or to go when they just didn't want to be at home. Although it was a small row house in the hood, it was decked out with the best furniture money could buy. It had soft, plush carpet running throughout the whole house, and there wasn't a room without a large flat-screen television mounted on the wall. There was even one in the bathroom. The living room had a cream sectional couch and glass end tables. In the dining room, there was a large, round marble table with three king-size chairs sitting around it. The chairs symbolized that everybody was equal. There wasn't a boss, nor was anybody better than another. At this table you were treated as a man, and that was it. No major conversation took place outside of this table, nor was there ever a time small talk occurred there.

Gutta dumped the contents of the duffle bag onto the table, threw the bag on the floor, and began counting the money. Everybody grabbed a section of the money and began counting. Not a word was said for the next ten minutes, and breaking the silence first was Zoe.

"I got $28,202," he said, leaning back in his chair. "Gutta, what made you take that bag of coins?" he asked jokingly, looking over at the quarters falling out of the small bag.

"I had time to. Shit, if I'd had fifteen more seconds, I would have taken the cuckoo clock off the wall in the manager's office."

"You did have extra time," Trust said, tossing the stopwatch onto the table in front of Gutta. The watch, counting minutes and seconds, said 1:17 on the nose, seventeen seconds over the established time the crew always worked with.

Gutta looked at the watch and was kind of disappointed with himself. He knew he was going to have to hear an earful from Trust behind it.

"Sixty seconds, Gutta. That's all we got to work wit'. You can't start straying from the course, because the moment you start doing that is the moment we go to jail. This isn't just your life you're playing wit'. It's all of our lives. This is the way we eat, and when I put a plan together, everything needs to be done precisely the way I tell you so that we can make it home."

"I know, I know. I just saw a safe inside the vault, and I wanted in. But you're right. I shouldn't have strayed from the course, and that's my bad."

"I wouldn't care if you saw an extra million lying around. If you can't grab it within sixty seconds, then you leave without it. Am I clear?" Trust asked, trying to regain some understanding about the rule within the circle.

Gutta was a little older than Trust and Zoe, and at the age of 34, he was in tip-top shape. He was the muscle of the crew. His ability to jump five feet onto a counter with one vertical leap, all the while carrying a gun and a duffle bag, was pretty impressive and useful. It came in handy when trying to stop the tellers from hitting any buttons under the counter without being seen. His aggression and body language made people think twice about trying to be a superhero. Gutta stood six feet two inches and weighed 230 pounds with a muscular build. His speed was also a plus, as was being able to get a lot of work done in a short period of time. Women often did a double take at his chestnut-colored skin and light brown eyes. He had a bald head and a full beard. Getting a woman out of her panties had never been a problem for him.

"I got $51,440," Trust announced, being the second to get finished counting his portion of the take.

"$44,330 and a bag of change," Gutta announced with somewhat of a smile on his face, looking at the bag of quarters. The other men couldn't help but chuckle at Gutta.

Trust raised a hundred-dollar bill in the air, and at
the same time, in sync with one another, they all yelled
out, "$123,972!" Everybody's math skills were sharp, and
counting the money was the joy of robbing the banks,
that was, after getting away. The money was quickly
divided up, each getting $41,324 apiece and letting Gutta
keep the bag of quarters.

Before getting up from the table, Trust threw a green
flag from his back pocket into the center of the table.
The green flag indicated that there was another job lined
up. If all three flags hit the table, then the job was to be
spoken about. If even one flag didn't reach the table, the
job wouldn't be talked about for weeks, or possibly even
a month. The thing about it was, nobody ever put off a
job before. Everybody was willing and trained to go at the
drop of a hat, no matter how much money they'd made
from the last hit.

Gutta and Zoe looked at each other briefly before tossing their flags onto the table. The curiosity of what Trust
had in store outweighed the money that was already
sitting in front of them. Trust pushed his money to the
side and began explaining.

"I got a job. It's a little more dangerous than the jobs
we've been doing. In fact, this by far is the most dangerous bank we've ever hit before. It's bigger, and it has
more than one way to get in and out. The two security
guards who walk the floor carry guns, and the traffic of
customers and employees is heavy during the morning.
The only way to get into the vault is by way of an eight-
digit PIN that only one of the tellers knows," Trust
explained.

"How many tellers are there?" Zoe asked, focused on
every detail coming out of Trust's mouth.

"There are eight tellers at the counter, two tellers on the floor dealing with loans, and a manager who sits in his office most of the time answering the phone," Trust explained.

"This job sounds like a fuckin' death trap, Trust," Gutta cut in. "These are the exact kinds of banks we try to stay away from."

"That's not even the half of it. The bank is in Center City, sitting on the corner of Broad Street."

Zoe and Gutta both put their heads in their hands and let out loud sighs. This was a nightmare, but neither man was willing to back out of it just yet. If Trust said he had a job to do, and he was sure about his work, more than likely the job was doable just as long as everybody played their part and did their jobs correctly.

"You must have a hell of a plan," Zoe said, breaking the silence in the room.

"Wait! Wait! Wait! What about the money?" Gutta asked before Trust could say another word.

"I'm glad you asked that, Gutta, because the amount of money we come out of there with is going to depend on us. The vault is the size of this house, and it has two levels to it. Downstairs is where they keep the cash, and on a regular day it can hold anywhere from $1 million to $1.5 million. Each teller would have about $15K to $20K at any given time. The upstairs holds the safety deposit boxes, which will also be accessible."

"What about the deposit boxes?" Zoe asked, curious as to how they were going to get inside of them.

"Well, I figure if we could give Gutta an extra sixty seconds and a master key to the boxes, he could do what he does best, clean out as many boxes as he can, and hopefully avoid coins and cuckoo clocks," Trust joked.

"What about the key to the vault? How will we know who got it? Because that could take up a lot of time," Gutta said, visualizing what he would do with a whole two minutes.

"Don't worry about that. I know exactly who got the key. All she wants is a small cut of the money and whatever is in deposit box 6-B. Whatever is in it is big enough to fit in your pocket."

"How can three men take over this large bank?" Zoe cut in.

"What about the getaway?" Gutta asked at the same time.

"The getaway is through the subway system. The bank is sitting right on top of the Broad and Walnut Street station. It connects to the Market Street El train and the Regional Rail trolley cars."

"How are we supposed to—"

"I get it, I get it," Gutta said, cutting Zoe off.

Zoe slammed his hand on the table hard enough to quiet everybody. He was a little more than frustrated at this point, and all he wanted was an answer to his question.

Zoe was considered to be the wild child of the crew. His position within it was the doorman, probably the second-most important job there was. He secured the outer perimeter of the bank as well as the inner. He scanned the premises for customers, employees, and police who may be entering the bank, and if they did, he would confront them immediately. Zoe was also known to be a shooter. If the police were ever tipped off and had the bank surrounded, Zoe was the type to try his hand and shoot it out with them. Hell, he was willing and ready to shoot anybody standing in the way of his freedom. At the age of 19, he was the youngest in the crew but was by far the most dangerous.

"How in the hell are we going to rob this big-ass bank with just the three of us?" Zoe asked, staring at Trust.

"I figure we do the job with four people. Two by the door, one working the floor, and one in the vault. I was thinking about bringing Amy along for this one. She could watch the other door."

Zoe and Gutta knew Amy well. She was Trust's old girl. Back in the day, Trust used Amy to set up big-time drug dealers so he could rob them for their drugs and money. Their relationship was tight, and up until two years ago they were inseparable. Although they weren't together as a couple anymore, they always stayed in contact and remained friends. Whenever Trust needed her, she was always there at the drop of a hat.

"So, when are we supposed to be doing the job?" Gutta asked, putting his money into his bag.

"Tuesday," Trust shot back with a serious look in his eyes.

"Tuesday!" Zoe said, surprised at how soon it was going down. "That's like five days away."

"I know, Zoe, but that's the least busy day of the week. There won't be that much traffic inside the bank. We got two minutes to get in and get out. Thirty seconds to get control of the floor, forty-five seconds to hit the vault downstairs, and thirty seconds to hit the safety deposit boxes upstairs. Once Gutta gets into the vault, I'll be cleaning out the tellers, so I'm gonna need you to watch my back," Trust said, looking at Zoe.

"Five days," Gutta said with a curious look on his face.

"Yeah, so that just means we got five days to go over the plan a little more extensively," Trust responded, pulling out his second green flag.

The second green flag meant that the job was a go, and it was pretty much locked in. The same rules applied as with the first set of flags. If all flags hit the table, then the job was getting done, but if just one flag didn't touch the table, the job was cancelled. Trust threw his onto the table first. Zoe and Gutta looked at each other, thinking that Trust was crazy as hell. But one thing about Trust that both men respected was that when Trust had a job lined up and a plan to get it done, nine times out of ten, it was going to be a success. Trust always kept in mind their safety, which was the most important thing. They relied on Trust in that aspect, and in all actuality, they trusted him with their lives, so it wasn't a surprise when the other two flags hit the table. That was it. And just like that, the job was locked in.

"You guys relax yourselves Friday and Saturday, but make sure we meet back here on Sunday so I can lay out the plan for us. Monday we'll go over it all day, so don't make any plans," Trust advised, grabbing his money off the table.

Trust was the brains of the crew. Not taking anything away from Zoe or Gutta, but when it came to robbing banks, Trust was a genius. All plans were thought up by him, and if he couldn't figure out a way to get away with the money, he wasn't going to do the job. He had staked out and cased banks for hours, timing everything like the moment they opened, when and which employees would show up first, what time they would close, and which employees were the last to leave. He would case the inside of the bank and take specific notes about the whole layout of the bank. He would take down names and races of the employees as well as exit routes and the closest backstreet to take so that he could avoid the highway as much as possible.

Robbing banks was the easy part. It was getting away with the money that counted, and getting away was what Trust specialized in. He was the best at it, and by the age of 24, he'd robbed some of the most secure banks on the outskirts of Philadelphia. He was smart, laid-back, cool, calm, and collected, but when it came to getting money, he was an animal.

Chapter Three

"Hey, bae." Erica looked up at Zoe as he entered their home. At 21, Erica was a little older than Zoe. Despite the fact that he was still in his teens, he was in her eyes very much a grown-ass man.

Erica was a stripper, and the deeper they got into their relationship, the more Zoe despised the fact that his girl shook her ass for a living. He never completely made her stop, because it was a fast-ass way to get money, and if nothing else, Zoe was a hustler. He made money in a lot of different ways, so he pretty much kept money in her pocket so she could keep the stripping down to a minimum. Zoe and Erica had been together for nine months, and she'd gone from stripping five nights a week to only two. Erica stood at five feet eight inches and had mahogany-colored skin. Her signature look was twenty-two-inch jet-black weave with a part down the middle. In all the time they'd been together, Zoe had seen Erica without the weave in her hair only twice.

"What's good?" Zoe greeted her as he gripped the strap of the duffle bag that was draped across his shoulder and sat down in his brown leather recliner. He unzipped the bag and pulled out two stacks of money. "Pay the rent tomorrow, buy some food, and then go shopping."

Erica smiled as she eyed the money while reaching out for it. Before she met Zoe, she loved stripping. It was a fun way to earn money and meet men, but now that she was in love, Erica didn't care about the club. Every time

Zoe came into the house and gave her money, she knew that was another day or two she could stay away from the club. When she met Zoe, he told her he was a hustler. Erica wasn't quite sure of all the ways he made money. She'd help him bag up weed and then, two weeks later, see him cooking up dope. All she knew was that Zoe got money. It didn't even really matter how.

Erica placed the money on the couch and screwed the top back on her bottle of nail polish. "You look tired, baby. You have a long day?"

Zoe let out a sigh. "Something like that. A nigga just ready to chill and relax." Zoe was a fan of working smart, not hard. He hadn't even planned on hitting another bank so soon, but fuck it. Until then, he was going to do what Trust told him to do: just chill. Zoe stood six feet even with caramel-colored skin and shoulder-length dreads. He had a baby face but a quick temper. If anyone underestimated him because of his looks, they'd more than likely end up regretting it.

Seeing the opportunity to cater to her man, Erica stood up and pulled her boy shorts out of her ass. "I'm about to roll you a nice, fat blunt. You can smoke while I suck you off, and then I'll bathe you while you sip Henny. After that, I'm going to put you to sleep," she stated with a devilish smirk.

"Damn," Zoe stated, looking up at her lustfully. His dick got hard as his eyes roamed her thick body.

Zoe had been getting girls since middle school. Even though Erica wasn't a lot older than him, she was the first grown-ass woman he'd ever dealt with. Most females his age only had their hands out for money or drugs. They ran the streets with their friends all day then wanted to party at night. Erica had times when she turned up, but as long as Zoe brought the money in, she catered to his every need.

Zoe found something to watch on TV while Erica rolled his blunt. As promised, as soon as she passed it to him and lit it, she was crawling in between his legs and freeing his dick from confinement. Holding his dick with one hand, Erica reached over and grabbed the glass of juice she'd been sipping on earlier. After taking a few big sips, she put the glass down and covered Zoe's dick with her cold mouth.

The sensation caused his stomach to cave in, and he let out a slight moan as Erica went to work on his dick. "Shit, ma," he hissed as she made every effort to deep throat him. Zoe's dick was huge, so huge that she threw up one night after trying to get all of him down her throat. "Do that shit," he encouraged her as she coated his dick with saliva.

Zoe grabbed Erica's hair and took a toke from his blunt. He felt like the man. Shit, fuck feeling like the man. He was the man.

"So, what do we have here?" a man dressed in a blue suit asked, walking into the Yellowstone Bank.

"Who are you?" a detective asked, sizing the man up with a curious look on his face.

The man looked around while reaching into his pocket to grab a cigarette, paying no attention to the question the detective just asked. He looked down on the detective and other police officers in the bank as if he were better than everybody in the room. Pulling out his badge, the man announced his position firmly.

"I'm Special Agent Ralley with the FBI," he stated, continuing his pursuit of dominating the locals. "I'm investigating a string of bank robberies all over the eastern district of Pennsylvania. I think it would be in everybody's best interest that you share what you got," Ralley said, leaning up against the teller booth.

"Well, we had three men with masks on carrying semi-automatic weapons. They stormed the bank, hit the tellers, and entered the vault. After cleaning it out, they put all the employees and customers inside then fled the bank, all within sixty seconds. The only things left were the coins in the tellers' registers and the bait money in the vault," the detective explained.

"What evidence have you recovered so far?" Ralley asked, continuing to look around the room.

"No hair, no sweat, no spit, no fingerprints, no nothing. Nobody in the bank could even identify the race of the men. They wore gloves, and the masks were draped over their necks. I tell you one thing; these guys are good."

"These guys aren't good!" Agent Ralley snapped, cutting the detective off in an aggressive manner. "As a matter of fact, what's your name?"

"Goodman, Detective Goodman."

Agent Ralley looked around the room, spotting the captain over by the door. He walked up to him and flashed his badge. "I want Detective Goodman removed from the crime scene," he demanded, and he wasn't taking no for an answer. "And if there is anybody else in here who thinks highly of these bank robbers, I suggest you remove yourself as well!" Ralley yelled out to all law enforcement in the room.

"Sir, a couple of customers reported that they heard motorcycles outside of the bank when the robbers left," a cop informed Ralley.

"Good. Now where is the video footage?" the agent asked, feeling like he was finally getting somewhere.

When the agent got to the manager's office, he got a chance to look at the footage and noticed that the robbers kept their masks on all the way up until they got onto their motorcycles, removing them as they pulled off. The way that the bikes were parked, the camera wasn't able to get a shot of any of their faces, nor the license plate numbers on the bikes. This made the agent even more angry and frustrated because it was another dead end. Ralley was so mad he got up and stormed out of the bank, bumping Detective Goodman on his way out.

Agent Ralley had been working these cases for about a year now, always ending up with the same results after robberies, which were no results at all. He was a veteran in the FBI, working the field for the past twenty years, but his old-school tactics were starting to get outdated for the modern-day criminals. The one thing that he wanted so badly was to be able to prove to his superiors that he wasn't ready to retire like everyone kept suggesting that he should. He hadn't had a partner for a couple of years, not because he couldn't find one, but because he didn't want one. Sometimes he didn't go strictly by the book, so having someone watching his back constantly would only slow him down.

With robbing one bank a month consistently and stealing no less than $100,000 each time with precise accuracy of execution, it was going to take a lot more than the tight restrictions of the FBI procedures to keep up and catch these mastermind bank robbers. Playing dirty was something that Agent Ralley was willing to do, and in fact he was already used to it.

Chapter Four

It was Friday morning, and Trust's phone had been ringing off the hook. God knows he needed some rest after all the running around he'd been doing all night, riding up and down the Broad Street Line, Market Street Line, and the Regional Rails. Now wasn't the time to be thinking about answering the phone.

"Baby, is everything okay?" Faith asked Trust, still half-asleep in the bed next to him.

"Yeah, I'm good."

"Come back to bed. You've been out all night," she moaned.

"Don't you have to go to work today?" Trust asked.

"I don't have to be at work until three," she replied, looking in the bathroom where Trust was sitting on the edge of the tub brushing his teeth. As tired as he was, he wasn't able to get back to sleep after the constant ringing of his phone, so he chose to get up.

Trust looked back into the room at Faith, admiring how beautiful she was lying there with her birthday suit on. "Come back to bed," she said, sitting up in the bed with nothing but the sheet covering the bottom of her breasts.

"If I come back into that bed, Faith, I promise you that you won't have to worry about making it to work today. You're gonna end up calling in sick fuckin wit' me," Trust joked.

Faith lay back on the bed, took the sheet off to expose
her body, and began playing with herself in front of
Trust. One hand was rubbing her clit while the other
hand grabbed a handful of her breast. She bit down on
her lower lip in pleasure as the juices began flowing
through her warm tunnel. It was hard for Trust to resist
something so beautiful lying in his bed.

"Come get it, daddy. Mommy is calling out sick today,"
she moaned, looking Trust in his eyes with a seductive
look decorating her pretty face.

Trust damn near choked on the toothpaste that was
in his mouth, and the show she was putting on gave him
movement down below. It wasn't long before he made
his way over to the bed, holding his rock-hard dick
in his hand. Faith pulled him on top of her and moaned
at the feeling of his dick penetrating her candy box. It
was so wet and juicy. Trust almost came within a few
strokes but quickly got himself together. He didn't beat
the pussy up like he started to but rather made love to
Faith slowly, deeply, and with passion.

Forty-five minutes and five strong orgasms later, Faith
curled up in the corner of the bed, holding her stomach
with one hand and sucking the thumb of her other hand
like a baby. Her pussy was swollen and thumping, and a
large wet spot in the middle of the bed marked the place
of a good time.

Trust's phone was still ringing off the hook, and it kept
on blaring until Trust turned it off and tossed it behind
the bed out of frustration. He thought about it for a
moment and knew that Zoe or Gutta might be calling.
Plus, he was waiting for Monica to call him, and that
was a phone call he couldn't miss. As soon as he reached
behind the bed to get the phone and turned it back on, it
started ringing again. Faith just chuckled to herself at
Trust looking down at the phone like it was some type

of alien. He looked at the number and saw that it was Monica, the bank teller.

"I have to take this call," Trust told Faith, getting up off the bed and going into the next room. "Yo, what's up?" Trust answered.

"Hey, it's Monica. I have been trying to call you all morning. I need to talk to you about that situation."

"Yeah, my bad. I was kind of doing something earlier when you called, but I'm good now, so what's up?" he shot back.

"We need to talk as soon as possible. Is there any way we can meet up today?" Monica asked.

"Well, I got a lot of running around to do today, but I'll be free later on if that's cool."

"That's good. Take down this address. I want you to come by my house later on around nine. I need you to bring something to write on, and don't forget to call me before you come. I don't know if my husband is going to be here," she said. She gave him the address then hung up.

Trust immediately dialed Amy's number, knowing that he had to make sure she was going to be down with the lick. As usual she picked up the phone within the first couple of rings. "How's my future husband?" she answered jokingly.

"What's good, beautiful? I need to holla at you about something. Where are you right now?"

"At work, but I go on my lunch break in about an hour. Come by the restaurant and meet me in the lunchroom if that's good for you."

Amy owned her own strip club in Center City, which turned into a great restaurant during the day. She was a go-getter, so she worked just as hard as her employees, serving food and washing dishes and not afraid of getting her hands dirty. At nighttime, it was a whole different ball game. She became a full-fledged businesswoman, watching over her dancers, hosting her rich clients, and financing the thousands of dollars her dancers made each night.

Trust went back into the room where Faith was attempting to fall asleep. Trust pretty much sealed the deal with Faith after making love to her for the second time. In this session, he gave her tough love, blowing her back out so he wouldn't have to hear from her for the rest of the day. She definitely was going to have to sleep it off.

Angela Bell washed her hands and eyed her reflection in the bathroom mirror before go her superior. She was being briefed on a new case, and ing to meet with she was excited. After two years of being an FBI agent, she loved her never-boring job. There had been a few rough months after a workplace romance with one of her colleagues went bad, but for the most part, Angela was over it. Standing five feet seven inches, with skin the color of toasted almonds, she got tired of people asking her why she was single. Her wide hips and round ass were a gift from her mother. No matter how much she worked out, the hips and ass wouldn't leave. Her body was toned, and she was in amazing shape. She loved wearing her natural hair in a mass of curls, and she had long lashes that she got complimented on often. It irritated her that since most people considered her beautiful, they acted as if they couldn't grasp that she was single. A lot of men even asked her what was wrong with her, and it was honestly quite disgusting.

Angela assumed that what was wrong with her was that she wanted an honest, loyal, handsome man to be truthful to her, have good credit and a stable source of income, and not have mad kids running around. It all seemed so simple, but that was far from the truth. Angela was a fuck-boy magnet and had sworn off dating. Since she had no kids and no man, she drowned herself in work. Her life consisted of late nights and early mornings, and for now, that was how she preferred it.

"Good morning." She smiled after entering the office of her boss. Carolyn Hodges could be irritating sometimes. Forget irritating, she could be a complete bitch, but it never bothered Angela too badly. She actually looked up to Carolyn. A black woman in the position she was in was admirable. With an office full of white men, the fact that a black woman was chosen to run the department made Angela proud.

"Good morning. The file I have for you to look over is for a guy by the name of Robert Green. Street name Gutta. The investigation has already been going on for a few weeks, and I need you to get caught up to speed. Fast. Officers are ready to make a move."

Angela gave a quick nod and opened the file. It was just another day in the life of an FBI agent.

Gutta and Zoe pulled up on Gutta's block only to see police lights everywhere flashing right in front of his house. He kept his cool and drove past the police cars as discreetly as he could. It was a good thing they were in Zoe's car, because had he been in his own car, they probably would have pulled him over immediately. Gutta knew that they could only be in there for one reason, and it wasn't his girlfriend, Wanda. His heart was racing, and under his breath he pleaded for them not to stop the car.

"Damn, dog, they got ya girl," Zoe said, seeing Wanda being brought down the steps in handcuffs. "What the hell is going on? Why the hell are they in ya crib like that?" Zoe asked curiously.

"I don't know, dog, but I know Wanda will call me as soon as she gets a chance."

"You don't think they know about the job we did, do you?" Zoe asked, thinking about the bank he and Gutta had robbed without Trust.

"Naw, dog, we did everything right," Gutta shot back at Zoe. "We'll find out in a couple of hours when Wanda calls me. Shit, they might even let her go, because she honestly doesn't know anything."

Before Gutta could get another word out, his phone started to ring. It got quiet in the car. Gutta looked down at the phone to see that it was a blocked number, which he normally wouldn't answer, but he had the feeling that it might be Wanda. "Yo," Gutta answered, looking out the window.

"It's me. I need you to come home right now," Wanda managed to get out from behind her tears.

Gutta couldn't believe what was coming from her mouth. She was trying to get him to come home so that the Feds could arrest him on the spot. He knew that they were still there because he could still see the lights flashing in front of his door from several blocks away where he had parked to get a clear view of the house.

Gutta looked at the phone as though he were talking face-to-face to Wanda. "Babe, you know I got mad love for you, right?" Gutta began in a disappointed voice. "I know the Feds are at the house right now, so you don't have to lie to me. All I want to know from you is if you know that they gonna lock me up the second I pull up at the front door," he said.

Wanda couldn't stop crying on the phone. She was crying because she was more embarrassed that her loyalty to Gutta was now in question. She did love Gutta, hands down, but this was the first time she ever came in contact with the FBI, and for whatever reason that was, she had no idea. All she knew was that they wanted to talk to Gutta.

"You want me to come home, Wanda?" Gutta said into the phone again.

"No," Wanda cried out over the phone. "No, baby, don't come home."

"That's my girl. Now put the agent who arrested you on the phone," he directed.

Gutta could hear Wanda crying in the background as a different voice appeared on the phone. It was shocking to Gutta that the voice belonged to a woman. He was expecting to talk to a man. She didn't even sound like a federal agent.

"This is Special Agent Bell," the woman said, waiting to hear the voice of the man she had been looking for.

"You sound kind of young to be an agent," Gutta teased. "Tell me, Agent Bell, why are you looking for me, and please don't tell me it's because I fell behind on my child support payments," he joked.

"Well, Gutta, maybe if you come in, we can talk about it. I can tell you that we do have a warrant for your arrest if that makes you feel any better. The longer you run, the worse things are going to get for you. I would hate to involve your girlfriend, but if you don't turn yourself in, we're going to have to hold her and possibly charge her for some of the things we found in your house."

Gutta had done so much dirt in the hood, he wasn't sure why they were looking for him: trafficking drugs, buying guns, robbing banks, credit card schemes, and more. It could have been anything. Just last week, Gutta and Zoe robbed a bank for $45,000 in New Jersey, then turned around and bought a kilo of cocaine all in the same day. He had a little neighborhood in North Philly where he sold drugs when he wasn't robbing banks. Whatever the Feds were looking for, it wasn't something light. But what he did know was that there was about a half brick of cocaine in the house and some weed. It definitely was enough to hold Wanda and charge her.

"Now you know you can't charge her with anything. She doesn't even know anything. Besides, her lawyer is my lawyer, and I never spent a day in jail because of him. In fact, this phone call is pretty much over. Catch me if you can," Gutta said then hung up the phone.

Agent Bell looked at the phone as Gutta hung up, thinking how arrogant he was even with his girlfriend in custody. One thing he said was true, and that was that the Feds really didn't want to charge Wanda with anything. Their focus was on Gutta and Gutta only. For now, they definitely were going to take her down to federal holding in order to ask her a few questions before letting her go.

"Ms. Wanda Simmons, what is your relationship to one Robert Lapheat Green, aka Gutta, and please don't be stupid enough to say you don't know who I'm talking about," FBI Agent Bell asked the minute she walked into the room where Wanda was sitting at a table with her nightgown on.

"Gutta is my boyfriend. We've been together for almost a year now," Wanda stated.

"What do you know about Gutta's drug business? Now before you answer that, I want you to think long and hard about your answer. This is not a game, Ms. Simmons. You don't talk, you go down with him," Agent Bell said, now walking around the room.

"Gutta does landscaping work for his money. I don't know anything about no drugs, Ms. Bell," Wanda lied.

"That's a three-hundred-thousand-dollar house you're living in that belongs to him. Gutta isn't that talented to landscape his way to the top. I took a look around the house, Wanda. There are a lot of very expensive toys in that house," the agent went on.

"I don't know what you're looking for, Agent Bell, but I was reminded on the phone about where my loyalty lies, and I'm sure I made it clear it wasn't with you. So, if you're going to charge me with anything, then do it. Otherwise, let me leave."

"Look, Wanda!" the agent began yelling and slapping the table with the folder. "Your boyfriend sold drugs to an undercover informant, and as soon as we catch him, his ass is going to jail!"

Before the agent could get another word in, another agent came into the room and stopped Bell from talking, ordering her to come into the hallway.

"What the hell are you doing?" Agent Rose yelled at Bell when she came into the hallway. "You're telling her the evidence we got on her boyfriend, and we can't even charge her with anything. She's being released in twenty minutes, and you're letting her leave with this kind of information."

"I know she knows more than what she's telling us, and if you give me a couple more hours, I think I can break her."

Agent Rose said, "She's to be released now instead of in twenty minutes, and you're not to ask her another question while she's here. Do I make myself clear? And, Agent Bell, you better hope you're still on this case by the end of the day. Now go in there and tell her she's free to go."

Bell walked back into the room where Wanda was, and before she could say anything, Wanda requested a lawyer. Bell looked at her with a fake grin on her face. "Well, Wanda, you won't need one of those right now, because you're free to go."

Without another word being said, Wanda got up and left the room. She didn't know what happened in the hallway, but she couldn't wait to get to the nearest phone so she could call Gutta. She knew Gutta sold drugs in Philadelphia, but she'd refused to give that information to the FBI in order to not get her man locked up.

Wanda stood on the elevator of the federal building, praying that Gutta wasn't angry with her. She'd been scared when the agents ran into the house. No matter if he was mad at her or not, she had to tell him what she knew. She owed him that much. She had no problem helping him spend his money when he brought it home, so she couldn't fold when shit got thick.

So many thoughts were running through Wanda's mind before she got out of the building. She thought about the fast life and all the money she and Gutta blew. She thought about the vacations they took, the expensive restaurants, the cars they drove, hers being a Range Rover and his being a Benz 600. She thought about the house he bought in Montgomery County for the both of them and how she warned him of the attention it would bring. Now, since the Feds were involved, Wanda could see the good in her life falling apart. But there was no way she wouldn't ride with Gutta 'til the end.

Chapter Five

Trust walked into the restaurant and saw Amy waiting on a customer. At first glance, she looked like she was a worker instead of the owner of the place. Looking around, all he could see were a bunch of rich white guys sitting around talking about stocks. There were a couple of lawyers sitting around quoting case law and bragging about what judges they knew personally. For a moment Trust felt a little out of place, but Amy suppressed his feelings when she attended to him like he was the president of the United States. Some of her customers watched and wondered who he was as she gave him the special attention.

"Hey, good looking. What can I do for you?" Amy asked, taking a seat in the chair next to Trust.

"I'm not the type to beat around the bush when we talk," Trust began. "I got a job on Tuesday, and it's worth about $1.5 million, give or take. It takes four people, and right now I only got three. I don't trust many people with my life, and that's why I'm coming to you. We split everything straight down the middle, so there's no need to ask how much you getting."

Amy looked at Trust and smiled. "You don't have to be so gangsta wit' me, boy. I know you better than anybody, so you don't have to be so hard when you talk to me."

"Look, if you changed ya life and you're not into it anymore, I can understand," Trust said, ignoring her last comment. "But I need to know something because I'm running out of time and people."

"You look around this place and think that I'm doing well, but the fact is I haven't been right since the day we broke up."

"Come on, babe, don't do me like that," Trust said, cutting her off. "You know I'm always here for you, but now ain't the time for that. I need to know if you're wit' me," he said, trying to stick to the reason he came there in the first place.

"You know, you always had a way with words, mister," she said, still smiling from ear to ear. "I hope you don't think these guys are paying the bills around here," she said, looking around at the lawyers and stockbrokers sitting around and only spending money on coffee and pound cake. "I got a business to run, so I know for sure that I can use the money. So yeah, you can count me in. Plus, I remember a time when we made a pact to always be there for each other no matter what, and I'm not about to go back on our word."

It was a relief. Trust really did need Amy for this job. She was already skilled in this field, thanks to Trust, and explaining her position wouldn't take much. He was truthful when he said that he didn't trust many people with his life. Amy was probably the only female besides his mother he would trust with his life, and that was big. She was thorough as hell and as gangsta as they came. Looking at her five-foot-five-inch frame and petite build, no one would ever guess that Amy could shoot with the best of them, and there wasn't a punk-ass bone in her body. When her white father left her black mother in the heart of the hood and they began to struggle, it was Trust who took her under his wing and taught her how to get money. When they were setting niggas up, he groomed her to be heartless. She was never to get attached to any of the men no matter how well they treated her, and she always was to be able to protect herself in case things got ugly.

"Call me tomorrow. We got to go over the plan on Sunday and Monday, so try to get as much rest as you can," Trust told Amy as he was getting up to leave. "You know I will never let anything happen to you?"

"You don't even have to explain," Amy said. "I already know that my life is in good hands. My only question is, do you want to try the dessert of the day? It's strawberry pound cake. It's soft, warm, and it tastes good."

Trust pulled a knot of money out of his pocket and eyed her as he placed it on the table. "No, thanks. I already had ya pound cake before, and it was a lot better than how you just described it," he said jokingly with a sexy smirk on his face. "All it's going to do is make me keep coming back for more, and right now, I really can't afford to take a bite out of that," he said, walking toward the door, leaving as smoothly as he came in.

When Trust left the restaurant, he got into his car, a blue 2018 Dodge Charger with a Hemi engine in it and pulled off with the sounds of "Fortunate" by Maxwell screaming out of the sunroof. He could depend on Amy to step up, and without her he probably wouldn't have done the job. She was smart and gifted with the talent of making good decisions at the drop of a hat.

Bell had been sitting there all afternoon going over Gutta's file, trying to get a better understanding of his criminal background so she could be prepared for their confrontation when it happened. She was pissed with herself after being chastised by her superior, and she refused to mess up again.

Gutta had been arrested a number of times in the past few years for multiple violent offenses. In February 2015, he was arrested for the attempted murder of his landlord for charging too much rent, and in September of the same year, he was arrested for beating a man halfway to death over a parking space. None of the victims testified in court, so the charges were dropped. The list went on and on all the way up to 2018, when he was charged with murder and won the case with a jury of twelve judging him.

Agent Bell sat at her desk looking over Gutta's file, trying to figure out if she was out of her league with Gutta, considering his rap sheet, but the small conversation she had with him over the phone intensified her desire to catch him. She also thought about the amount of information she had given to Wanda and hoped it wouldn't hurt her chances. Wanda was on her way home, and Bell knew the first person she was going to contact was Gutta.

Agent Rose walked into Bell's office and sat down, interrupting Bell's train of thought. "You know, I have been an agent for a very long time, and the one thing I learned in this field is that even the best criminals get caught eventually," Agent Rose said, twirling a pen in his fingers. "Don't take the job so personally, Agent Bell. After you catch him, there's going to be hundreds more just like him. Just get the job done, and make it home to your family," Agent Rose said.

"Well, Agent Rose, I have been chasing people like Gutta for a few years now, and I look at the neighborhoods they destroyed and the people they hurt in the process. These people sell drugs to kids and murder like it's legal. This is personal to me, and if a hundred more come behind him, then I'll take them personally too."

"The best advice I can give you right now is that you set up surveillance at his house and put a tap on the house phone. He's going to want to talk to Wanda to find out what she told you. If you stick to Wanda, you'll find Gutta," Agent Rose suggested. "Don't get caught up with that old-school saying, 'To catch a criminal, you have to think like a criminal.' In order to catch a criminal, you have to think better than a criminal," said Rose before getting up and leaving the room.

Trust walked up to the front door of Monica's house and rang the bell. In his pocket he clutched his pistol, not knowing if Monica's husband was going to be there. It was kind of weird how much of a rush she was in to see Trust, considering that they weren't supposed to meet up until Monday.

Monica came to the door with her bathrobe on and her hair still wet from the shower. Her breasts were barely covered, and Trust came to the conclusion that she'd timed her shower to coincide with his arrival on purpose.

"Come in," she said, stepping to the side. "You can come upstairs for a minute while I finish getting dressed," she told Trust while running up the stairs.

Damn, to be 40 years old, she got a body like a Coke bottle, Trust thought going up the stairs, following Monica to her bedroom. "You got big plans tonight?" Trust said, looking around the room at all the clothes lying out.

"Yeah. I have to meet my husband for dinner tonight. This might be the night we discuss our divorce," Monica said, not taking her eyes from the mirror. "I called you over here for two reasons, and the first one is to discuss the plan for Tuesday. Are you still ready for it?" she asked.

"Yeah, I'm still good. There's just a few things I need you to do during the robbery, and the first thing is never look at me or anybody else with guns. Act scared and don't say a word. The next thing I need to know is what the key looks like," Trust stated in a firm manner, not smiling or taking his eyes off of her.

Monica turned around and faced Trust. Unstrapping her robe, she let it fall to the floor. She stood there naked with a large key dangling from a string tied around her waist. The key looked like a credit card but larger, and it hung down around Monica's vagina.

"Oh, the second reason I called you here was because I want you to fuck me like you just came home from doing fifteen years in prison," Monica said, standing in front of Trust, playing with the key wrapped around her waist. "Then after you're done fucking me, I want you to fuck me again like you're about to go back for ten more years."

Monica's body was flawless. No stretch marks. No bruises. Her stomach was flat, and her breasts were perky. She was pretty in the face with light green eyes to match her brown skin tone. Her hair was so long it came down to her butt, and her lips were full and juicy.

Trust couldn't believe what Monica had just said to him, and he thought about the love he had for Faith and not wanting to cheat on her. All the women he could have had sex with outside of Faith were turned down because he knew that what he had at home was far greater.

"I can't do that," Trust said, looking at Monica's body. "I didn't come here for that, and besides, you're married."

Monica walked over to the bed and cleared the clothes off of it and lay down. "That wasn't a question, Trust. That was more of a demand," Monica said, lying back on one of the pillows. "You wouldn't let ya dick decide whether you do a million-dollar job, would you?" she said jokingly.

What the fuck is wrong wit' me? I got a bad bitch trying to give me some pussy for access to a safe with more than a million dollars inside of it. I love you, Faith, but daddy got to take one for the team.

Trust walked over to the bed and started to take his clothes off with only the thought of money making his dick hard. Sitting up in the bed, Monica took Trust's dick into her mouth, trying to swallow all eight and a half inches of it without choking. Her success showed because Trust had the look on his face like he was enjoying every minute of it. Grabbing her hair and pulling her face off his dick, Trust threw her back onto the bed and climbed on top of her like a lion on a zebra carcass. He slid his dick inside of her warm box. Monica moaned, loosening up her walls so he could put all of it inside of her. With every stroke, he went deeper inside of her, making her box fill with juice.

"Deeper, deeper!" Monica yelled out, biting on Trust's shoulder and holding on to his back.

While stroking her, Trust kissed her bottom lip and swiped his tongue against hers while grabbing a handful of breast. He snatched the key from around her waist and threw it across the room and started stroking Monica harder and harder, biting on her neck and growling in her ear.

Turning her over so she was on top, Trust reached up and grabbed her shoulders, pushing her body down on his dick. "Sit all the way on it," he told her, spreading her butt cheeks as she rode him.

Monica couldn't take it anymore. She was ready to explode sitting on his monster dick. "I'm cumming, I'm cumming!" she screamed out, bouncing up and down at a fast pace.

Monica's pussy tightened up as the orgasm made her body shake, and the juices from her box dripped down all over Trust's balls. Trust turned her back over onto her back and continued to stroke deeply and slowly, making Monica's orgasm last longer. After thirty-eight minutes of hard fucking and two minutes of making love, Monica was satisfied, still shaking with every touch that came from Trust.

With his dick still rock hard, Trust continued to stroke slowly. "I only fucked you like I just came home," Trust whispered in her ear. "Now I'ma fuck you like I'm going back to prison," Trust said while putting her in the doggie-style position.

Chapter Six

Wanda couldn't wait to call Gutta to tell him what the agent said to her. As soon as she got out of the federal building, she went straight to the phone booth to call him. *Please answer the phone,* she thought as the phone rang.

"Hello," Gutta answered the phone with an attitude.

"Hey, baby, it's me. I need to talk to you," Wanda whispered into the phone.

Gutta didn't forget about her trying to set him up to come home earlier and didn't really want to talk to her about anything. "Make it fast, Wanda. I'm not trying to be talking over this phone like that," Gutta said, trying to brush her off.

"Well, they just had me in the federal building, and the FBI agent said she was looking for you for drugs. She slipped up and told me that you sold some drugs to an undercover informant. I don't know how long they had you under investigation, but she asked me about the house and the cars."

"What did you tell 'em?" Gutta asked.

"I told them that you do landscaping for your money and that I didn't know anything about you selling drugs or anything. I told her I wanted a lawyer, but she let me go without charging me. I'm not sure, but I think they might be following me to see if I lead them to you. I'm not sure what to do or if I should go home."

Gutta just sat on the phone, not sure what to do about Wanda. He didn't know if he could trust her anymore, and he wasn't willing to risk going to jail to see her. Wanting to know more information, he stayed on the phone a little longer.

"What did they take out of the house?" Gutta asked Wanda with an attitude.

"They took the safe, some of your jewelry, and a couple of pots out of the kitchen. They also went into your closet. I'm not sure what they took, but they didn't come out empty-handed."

Gutta had a closet in his bedroom where it was big enough to walk in. It contained a couple of scales, two handguns, and some baggies to put his drugs in. Even though he didn't have drugs in the closet, there still was evidence that linked him to some type of drug activity. That concerned Gutta a lot on its own, but his main concern was the informant.

"Did they tell you who the informant was?" asked Gutta, trying to get all the information he could from Wanda.

"She didn't say, but another federal agent came in and stopped her from talking to me any further. Whoever it is, you got to know him."

"I want you to go home and wait for me to call you. Don't call me from the house phone. If you want to contact me, go buy a prepaid phone," Gutta said and hung up.

He turned to Zoe, who was sitting in the passenger seat of his car scrolling through his phone. "Dog, we got a rat on the block. The chick just told me the Feds said I served an informant."

"So, what you wanna do?" Zoe asked, now putting the phone down.

"Nothing. Don't worry about it. I think I know who it is, and if I'm right, you already know what happens next."

"You think we should give Trust a call and let him know what's goin' on?" Zoe asked. "You know we got to meet up with him on Sunday so we can get ready for the job."

"Yeah, I know. But no, we don't have to call him right now. I don't want him to get to worrying about nothin'. You know how he can get. I got to get some money ASAP. The Feds took like a hundred K from me today out of my safe. I got a couple dollars on the streets but not enough to go on the run," Gutta told Zoe.

"What about the rat the Feds got working for them?" Zoe shot back.

"I think it's the nigga named H. That nigga never sat well with me anyway. Plus, he was the only one I been selling big weight to for the past few months." Gutta pulled the gun from under his seat and put it on his lap. "I'm going to take care of my business wit' H, and I'll get back up with you a little later," Gutta said, now pulling up to his car, which was parked on one of the corners they ran.

As he got into his 600, Gutta looked over at the silver Chrysler 300 that was sitting on twenty-two-inch rims and had dark-tinted windows. Zoe never really drove his car because most of the time he was either with Gutta or he was sitting on the corner with his workers. Gutta thought about switching cars with Zoe for a couple days, knowing that his car would be hot right now.

"Yo, I need you to switch cars with me for tonight. Nobody knows ya car."

"You got it, dog. Just make sure you don't get a scratch on my car or this pretty Benz is mine," Zoe said, smiling but very serious. "You need me to roll wit' you?"

"Naw, young buck. Whenever I move out, I go solo so I can minimize witnesses. Always do ya dirt by yourself so nobody can ever point you out in court saying they saw you do anything," Gutta told Zoe, trying to school him to some game but at the same time turning over his keys to him in exchange for the 300.

It didn't take him long to arrive at his destination. Gutta pulled up and parked two blocks from where H and his boys sold drugs in the projects, located on Forty-sixth and Market Streets. There were a few different ways to get into the projects, but the back way was closer to the building H was in, so that was the way Gutta came in. Pulling a seventeen-shot Glock 9 mm from his waist, Gutta checked to make sure there was one in the head and then proceeded to one of the benches at the far end of the projects. Now it was a waiting game, because he wasn't sitting out in front of the building like he normally did, which made it hard to determine whether he was even in the area.

I knew this nigga wasn't right, Gutta thought, sitting on the bench and smoking a Dutch Master filled with Haze. *Every other day dis nigga come buy coke off me, and every time he came back to this dirty, old project. I haven't seen one crackhead come into or leave this building since I've been sitting here, and for him to buy between nine and eighteen ounces every other day, this building should be flooded with crackheads.*

Just then, H's car pulled up into the projects: a blue 1996 Crown Victoria with tinted windows. He got out of the car and went into the building, clutching a bag of food from McDonald's. Gutta tossed what was left of the Dutch and began walking toward the same building. The front door was jammed, so anybody could walk in or out without the door locking behind them.

Because it was nighttime, the guard didn't even notice Gutta coming into the building with a gun in his hand. Instead of taking the elevator, Gutta walked up the stairs, where there weren't any cameras, and made his way to the twelfth floor, where he remembered selling some drugs to H before. Gutta couldn't remember which apartment he'd gone into before, but it didn't matter, because as he reached the twelfth floor, he could hear H talking to a female by one of the apartment doors.

With his gun in hand, Gutta walked up behind H and put the gun to the back of his head. From where she was standing, the woman he was talking to didn't even know Gutta was there. Gutta grabbed H by his collar and pushed him into the apartment, knocking the woman over in the process and slamming the door behind him.

"Gutta, what's going on?" H said, now looking up at Gutta from the ground. The woman also lay on the ground, looking confused.

"I'ma ask you one time and one time only, and you better tell me the truth or I'ma blow your head clean off your shoulders," Gutta said, pointing the gun directly at H's head. "How long have you been working for the Feds?"

For a second, H didn't know what to do or say. Up until now, nobody had ever known about him working for the Feds, and it was a shock that Gutta had figured it out.

"For about two years now," H said, afraid of what Gutta was going to do but praying that he spared his life. "I wasn't going to come to court on you though. I was just trying to make some extra money on the side." H pleaded, "Please, please," as he saw the look in Gutta's eyes turn dark.

Before he could say another word, Gutta fired the first shot into the forehead of H, knocking his body to the ground. Five more shots went into his face, and eight went into his body. The girl started screaming and crying out, but she was silenced by two bullets entering her head as well.

Gutta walked back down the steps the same way he'd come up, only to be confronted by the guard at the booth. "Hey, you," the guard said, coming out of the booth, reaching for his nightstick.

"Hey, you," Gutta said back, pointing his gun at the guard, backing him up into the booth. "Where's the tape to the cameras?" Gutta demanded, shoving the guard into a chair.

The guard turned to the monitors and took the tape from the recorder, handing it over to Gutta. His cooperation was to no avail as Gutta fired his final bullet into the guard's head before leaving the building.

"Fucckkkkk," Zoe moaned as Erica deep throated his dick. She had the best head he'd ever had, hands down. Irritated that his phone was going off back-to-back, Zoe looked over at his phone to see that Trust was calling him. The head was so good he didn't want to answer the phone, but he knew it must be important because he called back-to-back.

"What's good, old head?" Zoe answered the phone with one hand, guiding Erica's head up and down on his dick with the other.

"Where are you at? I'm trying to holla at you," Trust said, driving down the streets of South Philly. "It's been a minute since we kicked it. I thought you might be willing to chill wit' ya old head tonight."

"Um, um, that sounds like a plan," Zoe said, pushing Erica's head deeper into his crotch.

"What the hell are you doing?" Trust said, hearing the change in his voice.

"Nothing," Zoe shot back, "Come get me. I'm in the crib. Beep your horn when you get here." As soon as Zoe hung up the phone, he heard a horn beep. Trust had already been on the way to the crib when he was calling. Just to make sure he heard right, he called Trust.

Trust looked at his phone. It was Zoe calling. "Yeah, that's me, young buck. Come on outside," Trust said, sitting in front of Zoe's house.

"Give me about five minutes," Zoe said in a strained voice. Erica did something with her mouth that made him instantly cum down her throat. Zoe ended the call and looked over at Erica in amazement. "What in the hell was that?"

"What?" she giggled as she acted like she didn't know what he was talking about.

Zoe continued to look at her in awe. "Goddamn, ma, you're dangerous as hell. Peep this though, I gotta make a run with Trust. I'll be back." He instantly saw the disappointment on Erica's face. "I promise as soon as I make it back in the crib, I'm sliding this fat dick all up in you, ma. Yo' ass gon' be walking funny tomorrow."

Erica gave Zoe a small smile. She tried not to bitch too much about him running the streets, but sometimes it got annoying. She just tried to remind herself that him running the streets was what took care of them. She had hoped to have a serious conversation with Zoe after they had sex, but as usual, something came up. They for sure needed money, because once she told him what she had to tell him, he would for sure put an end to her stripping days. Erica just didn't know how they could raise a child together with the lifestyle he lived. Shit, she wasn't even sure if Zoe wanted a child.

"I Can Feel It in the Air" by the Broad Street Bully was playing in Trust's car when Zoe stepped out of the door, fixing his clothes. It'd been a couple of weeks since Trust sat down and talked to Zoe, which was something he had done ever since he took him under his wing. Even though Trust only had him by five years, Zoe looked up to Trust as somewhat of a father figure because Trust had an old soul. Wise, smart, and full of knowledge, Trust took the time to school Zoe on a daily basis as he grew to be a man. Trust would take a bullet for Zoe at any given time of the day, and Zoe would do the same for him.

"What's good, old head?" Zoe said, extending his hand for a shake when he got in the car. "Good old Faith let you come outside tonight," he joked.

"Let me tell you som'n, young buck: if you think a woman can't be the boss too, imagine if not one woman in the world would give you pussy unless you did what they told you to do. I bet my bottom dollar you'd comply."

"Old head, you always got some shit wit' you. Where are you taking me tonight? I got to get back home and figure something out with my girl," Zoe said, thinking about what Erica did to him before he left.

Trust started laughing because he knew that, from the way he said it, it was concerning sex. "So, what have you been doing with yourself, Zoe?"

"I've been chillin', trying to stay out of trouble. You know me, ride around all day fuckin' with bitches and kicking it with a couple of homies."

"What about you and Gutta? You messing with that drug shit, too? You know not all money is good money," Trust went on. "You got to be smart out here, man, because if you aren't, you know where you're going to end up, right?"

"Dead or in jail," Zoe answered. "I do a little bit but nothing too major. For the most part, I do a lot of taxing in my hood. A nickel bag gets sold on the block, nigga, I want in."

"Yeah, that's cool for now, but you got to think about ya future, Zoe. I hope you been saving money from all these jobs we done."

"Naw. I got a couple grand saved up for a rainy day, but I could do a lot better, and I will."

"Look, Zoe, I love you like we came from the same mother, and all I want is the best for you. I don't want you being like Gutta. He's good when it comes to robbing banks, but the stuff he does on the streets draws a lot of attention, and if he draws it to himself, he's drawing the same attention to us, ya dig? I don't got love for Gutta like I got for you. Just like I said, he's cool, but eventually I got to get rid of dead weight. I got about three more jobs lined up for us, then after that I'm done."

"Damn, old head, you doing it like that?" Zoe said, really amazed that Trust was ready to quit. "Let me hold something, big baller," Zoe shot at him.

"I ain't gonna turn you into no flatfoot hustler. You better start stackin' ya money, and I'm not talkin' about a couple of grand for a rainy day." Trust pulled up in front of Amy's strip club. "You might be too young to come up in here," he said, smiling at Zoe, knowing he was only 19.

"Oh, yeah?" Zoe said, getting out of the car. "Let me show you how I get down."

In the club, there were lawyers, stockbrokers, and different types of businessmen who made it rain five- to twenty-dollar bills on the strippers. As soon as Trust and Zoe walked through the doors, all eyes were on them, and not the eyes of the fellas, but all female eyes.

"There are my two favorite men," Amy said, coming to meet Trust and Zoe at the door with three nice dancers with her. "I got ya VIP room ready, Zoe," Amy said, not even looking at Trust.

"Naw, I'm good. I'm here with Trust tonight. Give us a room together, two bottles of Ace of Spades, and four dancers," Zoe demanded, passing Amy a wad of money.

Trust looked at Zoe and just smiled. At first, Amy was giving Zoe all the attention, but she came to her senses when she gave Trust a hug and a kiss and held his hand going to the VIP room. The customers never saw Amy dance before, but when Trust came into the building, she became someone else. Guys were whispering to each other, "Who the hell is this guy? He must be a rapper or something." They couldn't understand why he was getting all the attention when they were high rollers.

"Take a look around, Zoe," Trust said, pointing out the different groups in the club. "You got ya bankers, ya lawyers, ya stockbrokers, ya politicians, ya drug dealers, ya college boys, and then you got us," Trust went on. "Everybody in here got one thing in common, and that's money. Even the dancers are about money. Look at 'em," Trust said, pointing at the girls dancing in front of them. "The only difference between them and us is how fast we get our money. It could take them years to make a million dollars, but for us, we can do it in months and with less work. I need you to get real focused, Zoe. Our way of life doesn't last forever, so you got to plan your exit. Me, I'm done, young buck. After the fall, I'm going into retirement, ya dig? I can't tell you what to do with your life, and if you decide to keep going, that's your business. You're grown. But what I will tell you is that if you do decide to keep robbing banks, let me give you the game on how to get it done right so you won't go to jail."

"I thought about doing my own thing, but you know my loyalty is with you, and I would never go behind ya back," Zoe said, popping open a bottle of Ace of Spades. "Shit, I don't know how you come up with these plans, but however you do it, I know I can't do it like that."

"Look, I'll make a deal with you," Trust went on, now looking Zoe in the eyes. "I'll give you the game and all the tools you need if you can give me ya word that you won't rob another bank after the day you turn twenty-one. By then you should be one of the richest people in Philly."

Zoe thought about it for a second. Anything he gave his word on with Trust, he always made sure he could stand on it. He had a great deal of respect for Trust, and he'd never lied to him because of the love he had for him. "Yeah, I'll give you that. You got my word that I won't rob another bank after I turn twenty-one."

"Is that ya word?" Trust asked.

"You of all people should know that when I give my word on something, it's as good as gold," Zoe shot back, looking Trust in the eyes, raising his bottle of Ace of Spades in the air so he could touch the glass.

Trust and Zoe sat in VIP watching the dancers go crazy. One of them was dancing on the table in front of them, when from out of nowhere, she bent straight over, grabbed her ankle with one hand, and then pulled from her pussy a string of golf ball–size pearls. Her pussy was so wet you could see drops of juice falling off every ball as it came out.

"Faith would kill you if she knew you were in here watching this," Zoe joked.

"Young buck, you just don't know. I been going hard all night," Trust said, thinking about what he had to do to Monica for that key. "You either go hard or go home, Zoe. You either go hard or go home."

Chapter Seven

Angela's mouth fell open as she let out a slight moan and arched her back as she prepared to reach her peak. "Ummmmmmmm." Her body jerked as she came long and hard.

Angela's phone rang, and she let out a small sigh. She couldn't even enjoy the aftermath of an orgasm without her phone ringing. Turning her vibrator off and opening her eyes, she saw that it was her job. These days, her phone only rang if her parents, sister, or her job were calling. Angela tried not to get depressed as it hit her that she really didn't have a life outside of her career. It looked like she was going to be one of those women: no husband, no kids, nothing fulfilling. Just a nice home, expensive car, and a nightstand full of vibrators.

Angela answered her phone, and after a few seconds of listening, she assured her superior that she was on the way. If she couldn't be lucky in love, she could for damn sure be good at what she did for a living.

An hour later, Agent Bell stepped over H's body as she entered the apartment. Detectives were taking pictures and collecting any evidence they thought might be useful for the case. Some cops were in the kitchen, on the balcony, and in the bathroom, and a small group was in the bedroom down the hall.

Flashing her badge at one of the detectives, Bell took a deep breath. "What do you have so far?" she asked the detective, looking down at H with bullet holes everywhere.

"One male, one female shot to death. The male was shot once in the head, five times in the face, and it looks like seven or eight more times in the chest area, all close range. The girl was hit twice in the head. She didn't even feel the second shot," the detective informed her.

"What kind of evidence did you find?" Bell asked.

"Well, I got sixteen shell casings, and that's pretty much it. No prints but the girl's because she lives here. All of the male's money is still in his pocket, and nothing seems to be taken from the apartment. This looks personal," the detective said, snapping another photo of the bodies.

"Yeah, he really cleaned up after himself," Bell said, talking about the dead guard downstairs and the tapes from the monitor being missing. The first person Bell thought about was Gutta and how she gave hints to his girlfriend about the informant. "Who's in the back room?" Bell asked, noticing the gathering of police.

"That may be the only key to this case. The niece of the deceased woman was in the back room the whole time when they were being killed. She said she got a look at who it was but not a good look."

"How old is she?"

"Seventeen. Sad she had to witness the murder," the detective said before walking out.

Agent Bell walked into the back room to see a couple of rookie detectives showing the girl some photos. The girl looked scared and confused and couldn't stop crying. If this little girl could point out Gutta in a photo lineup, that would be all she needed to charge Gutta not only for drugs, but for a triple homicide on top of that. Bell wasn't about to let the young detectives mess up her opportunity by interrogating a child and scaring her half to death.

"Back up, back up," Bell said, walking into the pack of lions surrounding the girl. "This is going to be a federal case," she said, flashing her badge to the rest of the police in the room. "I appreciate your help, boys, but you can stop asking questions now. Look at the girl. She's scared," Bell said, grabbing the girl by the hand and walking her out of the room, covering her eyes as they stepped over the bodies on their way out the apartment door. "We're going to get you home to your parents. Where do you live?"

"I live in the building next door. My mom is at work, and my dad is in jail," the girl answered.

"Well, what is your name?"

"My name is Jasmine. I just want to go home," she cried out.

"Don't worry. My name is Special Agent Bell. I'm going to make sure I get the person who did this to your aunt, but I'm going to need your help. First I gotta get you home safe, and then we can talk there. Trust me, I'm not going to let nothing happen to you. You're now protected by the FBI," Bell told Jasmine as she escorted her to the next building.

"An hour tops, Faith," Trust warned her as he pulled up to Barbie's home. Because he had such an important job lined up, along with the fact that he hated Barbie, that was enough for him to tell Faith there was no way in hell that he was coming to her engagement party. *Fuck Barbie's bitch ass,* was how he felt.

"That's fine, Trust," Faith assured him. She was done trying to get Trust to like Barbie when, some days, she didn't even like the woman herself. She couldn't blow off her engagement party, however.

Barbie had been gloating for the past few days after Clinton proposed to her on a dinner date. She threw together an engagement party in record time. Barbie managed to rent out a small venue, and when Faith walked in, she was quite impressed. The decor was gold and black. There were balloons everywhere and huge ten-by-thirteen photos of Barbie and Clinton in black frames. There was an array of food and even a three-tiered cake. Everything was elaborate and done in true Barbie fashion.

Faith didn't see Barbie as soon as she walked in, so she greeted the people she did know, like Barbie's parents and Elaine. A waiter walking by with a tray filled with champagne flutes offered Faith and Trust drinks.

"Where is Barbie?" Faith asked Elaine after taking a sip of her drink.

"Toward the back taking pictures."

"How long have you been here?"

"About ten minutes. And I'll be leaving probably in another thirty."

That was no surprise to Faith. Most people had to take Barbie in small doses.

"Faith," Barbie squealed, rushing over to her friend.

Faith opened her arms for a hug just as Trust's body grew warm. The man hot on Barbie's trail had to be her fiancé. The problem was that Trust had seen him before. This nigga was the manager of the last bank they hit. Though his face was covered and there was no way the man could have known who he was, Trust was still uncomfortable.

"Baby, you know Faith," Barbie said, touching Clinton's arm. "And this is her boyfriend, Trust."

Clinton smiled and extended his hand for a shake. Rather than speaking, Trust just gave him a smile and a brief nod. It was going to be a long-ass night. He felt that he would be okay, however. He would just keep his talking to a minimum. Clinton surely talked to people every day. There was nothing about his voice that was that memorable. As long as he remained confident and didn't start acting suspicious, everything should be all good. To his relief, Barbie's parents called her and Clinton over, and Trust didn't have to worry about conversation with them.

"See? That wasn't so bad, was it?" Faith turned to him with a smile.

"Nah, it wasn't. But I have a long day ahead of me tomorrow, and I still want to be going soon."

Faith gave a slight nod. "What exactly are you doing tomorrow?" she inquired after taking a sip of wine. It may not have been the best time to pry, but it was normal to ask these kinds of questions in a relationship. Faith talked Trust's head off every day about things that went on at the hospital.

Trust didn't miss a beat. "I have to meet with the owner of a property I'm thinking about buying. The previous owner died and left the estate to her son out in California. He's not interested in having to maintain it. Also, I have to go to the store and meet with contractors about fixing a leak in the roof."

Faith felt bad for ever doubting him. Trust worked hard. He was a respectable businessman, and she was proud of him. "Okay, baby. Another thirty minutes and we can leave."

Chapter Eight

Pulling up to the First Bank, Trust, Gutta, Zoe, and Amy hopped out of two Yukon Denali trucks with the letters FBI on the back of their jackets and semiautomatic handguns in their hands. Amy and Zoe went to the back door, entering it with the security guard at gunpoint. Once inside, Zoe jammed the door behind him so nobody would be able to come in or go out.

Trust and Gutta came through the front door at the same time with Gutta hitting the guard in the back of his head, making him fall to the ground. While Gutta zip-tied the guard, Trust went into the middle of the floor, where people still didn't know what was going on.

"Everybody put ya hands in the air!" Trust yelled, firing two shots into the air and then pointing the gun at the tellers so they'd back off from their booths. "You push your button, I'll push mine," he said to the tellers.

Amy yelled over to Trust that her door was secured as well as the guard, while Zoe made his way over to the front door. Seeing one of the bank staff trying to slip away into an office, Amy walked up beside him before he could get in the door, grabbed him, and threw him to the floor on his face.

"Secured!" Trust yelled out, indicating that Gutta was up. "Two minutes!" he screamed, looking down at his watch as Gutta jumped over the teller's counter and grabbed Monica first. He snatched the key from around her neck as the other tellers watched on, shocked and scared for their lives.

None of the people in the bank moved from where they were standing, and some were still confused by the FBI jackets the robbers were wearing. They didn't know if this was serious or just a drill, but they weren't moving just in case. Gutta started on the downstairs level, shoving large bills into his duffle bag at high speed. The more money he saw, the faster he moved to get it all in the bag without bagging any dye packs with it.

"One minute, forty-five seconds!" Trust yelled out, looking around the room.

Filling up one of the bags, Gutta ran out of the vault and handed it to Amy at the back door. He quickly ran back into the vault and began filling another bag with the smaller bills he left behind.

"One minute, thirty seconds!" Trust yelled, now pulling a trash bag out of his jacket, going to each teller's booth and stuffing the money in the bag.

Gutta made his way to the second level of the vault and began opening the boxes starting with B-6, the box Monica wanted the contents of. When Gutta opened the box, he saw a black bag and a few pieces of paper in it. He just grabbed the bag and put it in his back pocket, then started working on a couple of boxes around it. B-1, B-2, C-1, C-2. He just popped away and emptied the contents into the bag without even looking to see what was in the boxes.

"Forty-five seconds!" Trust yelled out, walking up to Monica's register, which was the second-to-last register to be emptied. Trust caught the look in Monica's eyes as she looked from him to the teller's register next to hers, indicating that she'd hit the button. Trust looked and saw the light on under her counter, blinking. He looked at the white lady sitting in the chair with her hands on top of her head and her eyes full of tears.

"I'm sorry," she said to Trust as the tears started coming down.

"We got to go! We got to go now! Now! Now!" Trust yelled out so Gutta could hear him. "Code red! Code red!" he yelled again, meaning somebody had pushed the alarm.

Gutta stopped what he was doing and left the vault with the second bag that was mostly full. Amy made her way to the front door, dropping smoke bombs as she crossed the lobby, making the air fill up with thick green smoke.

The first two out of the bank were Amy and Zoe, who made their way down the subway tunnel right next to the bank, peeling off the FBI jackets they had on. Amy heard the sounds of police cars and hesitated for a second, debating whether to go back for Trust, but she continued to move knowing he would be right behind her.

Before leaving the bank, Trust walked up to the teller who had pushed the button and shot her twice in her legs. Gutta walked out first, only to see a cop car pulling up. Without a second thought, Gutta began shooting at the cop car, striking the driver in the chest, only dazing him because he had a vest on.

Trust came out of the door too, dropping several smoke bombs, filling the outside air with the same thick green smoke before firing six shots into the passenger side of the police car. The air was so thick with smoke that Gutta could barely see the entrance to the tunnel, but he managed to stumble down the steps with Trust right behind him. Looking at their watches, Trust and Gutta made their way down the tunnel toward the stations where the El, trolleys, and subways were running.

Gutta branched off and walked to the trolleys at the Fifteenth Street station where he saw Zoe getting on the first trolley. The second trolley pulled right up on time for Gutta to get on. On the trolley with the duffle bag, Gutta sat all the way in the back of the car by the window, checking to see if anybody was behind him as the trolley pulled off.

Feeling discomfort in his back pocket, Gutta pulled the little black bag from box B-6 out to check what was inside. He looked into the bag, and his mouth dropped to the floor when he saw that it was full of diamonds. He poured a couple into his hand and got a better look at the mothball-size rocks in the bag. He pressed one against the window of the trolley and cut a line straight through it.

"I see why Monica wanted what was in B-6," Gutta mumbled to himself. "Girl's best friend, huh?"

Meanwhile, Trust walked up to the El train, where he caught up with Amy standing on the platform with the duffle bag on her shoulder. Behind her was a SEPTA cop trying to listen to what was being said over his walkie-talkie.

"Suspects posing as FBI on foot," was what came over the officer's radio, and standing right in front of him was a female clutching a jacket with the initials FBI showing. The cop reached for his gun but was stopped by Trust sticking his gun in his ribs and grabbing the gun from his holster.

"Do what I say and nothing less, or I promise you this will be your last day working," Trust told the cop. "Close your eyes and don't turn around," he said, taking the walkie-talkie and handcuffs off the cop and placing the cuffs on his wrist. He wasted no time cuffing the cop to the bench. "Keep your eyes closed for two minutes before you open them, and don't think about uncuffing yourself, because I got the key," Trust said.

Trust grabbed Amy's arm and led her down to the subway, hoping the cop thought they got onto the El train that was pulling up as they were walking off. Trust took the bag off Amy, grabbed her hand, and got on the Broad

Street subway, which was his plan B in case something went wrong. Getting off a few stops later, Trust flagged down a cab that was passing by.

"You're so handsome when you get in gangsta mode," Amy said, smiling at Trust as they got into the back seat of the cab. "It feels like the good old days rolling out with you today," she said, putting her hand on top of his.

The whole way back to the hideout, Amy and Trust talked as if nothing had just happened, but for them, it was nothing new. They'd been here many times before, taking down big scores back in the day when they were together as a couple. Today only brought back some good memories that had Amy feeling the way she did now.

"Pull over right here," Trust said to the cab driver, telling him to stop six blocks away from the hideout so the cabby couldn't get an idea of where they were going.

When they got into the house, Gutta was sitting at the round table, clapping two large stacks of money together at a well put-together plan by Trust. He had already begun celebrating with a Dutch full of haze in his mouth and a bottle of champagne sitting in a bucket of ice. Everyone was in the house but Zoe, which quickly caught the attention of Trust.

"Where's Zoe?" Trust asked, not yet ready to celebrate.

"He didn't get back yet. I saw him get on the trolley right before I did. He should be here any minute now."

Trust headed for the door with his gun on his waist in an attempt to go find Zoe, but he stopped at the front door when Zoe came running up the steps. Coming into the house, Zoe didn't say a word and went directly to the TV, turning it on to the news station. Nobody in the room had any idea what was going on, and everyone was silent until the news came back on from the commercials.

"This just in," the anchor started. "Police are on a manhunt for a suspect in a triple murder two nights ago.

This man, Robert Green of North Philadelphia, is wanted for questioning in a fatal shooting in West Philadelphia late Saturday night."

As the anchorman continued to talk about the murder, a giant photo of Gutta took up the TV screen, making everybody's mouth drop to the floor. Trust was furious, and the only thing he could think about was who might have seen Gutta come into the house. This was exactly the kind of attention Trust was talking about with Zoe the other night in the club.

Trust walked up to Gutta and began swinging, punching him in the face, never giving Gutta the chance to get up. He knocked him out of the chair, then got on top of him and kept on punching Gutta in his face with his right fist and then left and back again. Gutta finally got up enough strength to fight his way back to his feet, then tried to reach for his gun on the table. He was denied when Zoe grabbed it first. Seeing his intention, Trust pulled his gun from his waist and pointed it at Gutta's face.

Everybody got quiet and nobody made a move. The air was so thick you could cut it with a butter knife. Trust moved the gun from his face and passed it to Amy to hold while he continued to beat Gutta's face in with his hands. It wasn't an easy fight for Trust, because Gutta knew how to fight as well, but it was no match at the end.

When it was all said and done, Gutta sat in one chair and Trust sat in the other chair, facing each other, trying to catch their breath. With a black eye and a busted mouth, Gutta wiped the blood from his face with a washrag handed to him by Amy. Although Trust didn't have love for Gutta like he had for Zoe, he still didn't want anything bad to happen to him.

"We have to get you out of the city," Trust managed to get out as he took deep breaths. "This is the reason I told you to leave the drug game alone while you were still on this crew. Whether you know it or not, you jeopardized everybody in this room."

"I know. That's my fault, y'all. I fucked up. Give me 'til the end of the night and I'm gone. Right now I really need y'all help if I'm gonna make it out the city. I got . . ." Gutta thought about telling them about the diamonds but caught himself midstream.

"Right now, we got to sit down and count this money," Trust said, heading over to the round table with the second duffle bag and the trash bag of money from the tellers. "While we count this money, you're going to explain to everyone why the hell yo' picture is on the TV for a triple murder in West Philly, and please, whatever you do, just keep it real with us, ya dig?"

Agent Ralley came storming into the First Bank with five other agents following him, pointing and demanding answers like a madman. He was moving as if he was in a rush to preserve any evidence left behind.

"I want all the customers on the left side of the floor and all employees on the right. Nobody leaves this bank without being interviewed by me or by one of my staff," he announced in the middle of the floor. "All physical evidence is to be reported to Agent Barkely. Who's the manager? I want to see the person in charge."

Agent Ralley was on fire and determined to see if the crew he was looking for was in fact responsible for this robbery. If they were, who was their fourth member? Up until now they'd only worked with three people.

"Ralley, the manager is waiting for you in his office," another agent came over and told him. "I think you might want to hear what he has to say, too. You're not going to believe this."

Ralley walked into the office, and sitting in the chair was a middle-aged white man, half bald and wearing a tacky suit. He was still kind of shaken up from the robbery but was more than willing to talk.

"I'm sure you got an amount of money that's missing," Ralley began.

"Well, Agent Ralley, that's why I called you in here. About the money, as of now we've calculated a little over a million in cash, but he also opened a few safety deposit boxes in the vault."

"How much did he get from there?"

"What I'm about to tell you cannot leave this room under any circumstances," the manager said with a slight hint of fear in his eyes. "Among other jewelry taken, there were some diamonds stolen as well."

"Diamonds? What kind of diamonds?"

"The kind that are worth twenty million dollars. I have to contact the owner to inform him of the theft, but I want to assure you that finding these diamonds should be first priority on the FBI's to-do list."

"Who knew about the diamonds?"

"The owner of the bank branch, myself, and the key-card holder."

"What the hell is a key-card holder?"

"Every few years, the bank chooses a teller to hold the key to the vault so, in case of a robbery, nobody, not even the manager, would have access to the deposit boxes except this key-card holder. None of the other tellers knew that this person possessed it. It's a security measure the bank takes to ensure that the property of our customers will be safe."

"It's a dumb one. Where's the teller who's in charge of the key?"

"Monica Fields. She's the only black teller but the most trustworthy of them all."

Agent Ralley still couldn't believe what the manager told him about the diamonds. He now became more interested in this case whether it was the crew he was looking for or not.

Monica was sitting in a chair at a table along with the rest of the employees when Agent Ralley walked up and identified himself. Monica sat there with a blank look on her face as if nothing had just happened.

Agent Cook walked up next to Ralley, whispering in his ear, interrupting the start of Ralley's questions. "I spoke to a couple of the tellers before you walked up, even the one who got shot, and they all said the robbers went straight for her like they knew she was the one with the key. The teller who got shot also said that it looked like she tipped one of the robbers off about the silent alarm."

It was like Agent Ralley could taste blood in his mouth, looking down on a sheep like a wolf. He asked Monica to join him in one of the offices the police used to question everybody in. Once inside the room, Ralley sat on top of the desk and looked down at Monica, who was sitting in a chair a couple of feet away from him. He started off with small questions like how long she had been working at the bank or if she had seen any of the robbers' faces. Basic questions got basic answers from Monica. She'd expected these types of questions and showed no signs of fear all the way up until Agent Ralley got a little slicker with his questions, making it tougher for Monica to answer them.

"How is it that out of all eight tellers working here today, the robbers knew exactly who to go to for the key to the deposit boxes?" Ralley yelled, now loosening his tie.

The sweat started dripping down her underarms from the first major question. "I don't know why they came to me out of everybody," she stuttered.

The questions didn't stop and neither did Monica with her shaky answers. After seeing he wasn't getting anywhere sitting in this office, Ralley asked Monica to come down to the federal building for further questioning, and she reluctantly complied. She requested to take her own car instead of riding with Ralley, but when her request was denied and she was told she had to ride with him, she knew in her gut that something had gone wrong.

Oh, my God. I'm about to go to jail, Monica thought, walking toward Ralley's car. She hadn't thought anybody was going to get hurt, and she damn sure hadn't thought that the FBI was going to question her the way they were about to. All she could think about was calling Trust to see if he had gotten the diamonds. She needed to do it quickly before Trust found out the value of them, because if he did, she probably would never see him again.

Chapter Nine

When Zoe entered his home, he found Erica in the kitchen cooking. She was dressed only in black boy shorts and a black sports bra. Zoe placed the duffel bag containing his cut on the kitchen table. "You may as well quit that fuck-ass job at the strip club, 'cause ya nigga got you," he stated, eyeing her plump ass. It seemed to have gotten bigger over the past few weeks, and Zoe had made up his mind. He didn't want anyone else eyeing what he had.

Erica turned around and eyed Zoe as she leaned up against the stove. "Are you finally going to be here for at least ten minutes without answering the phone, running back out, or falling asleep? I have something I need to talk to you about."

Zoe raised an eyebrow as his eyes roamed over Erica's face. She normally wasn't one to trip about him running the streets. He hoped she didn't pick today of all days to badger him, because he wasn't really in the mood.

"I'm standing here, ain't I? You could've just spit it out already. You already know why I'm in the streets a lot. This," Zoe stated as he raised his duffel bag high in the air.

"Yeah, well, I'm pregnant, and the thought of me having to do everything alone is scary. Will you have time to go with me to appointments, change a diaper, or even hold the baby?" Erica asked, half-serious and half-joking. She really was nervous, and Zoe could see it in her eyes.

He stood speechless for a second. They had sex all the time, but for some reason, he was still shocked to hear the words "I'm pregnant" come from her mouth. Zoe was young, but he knew enough to know that way more came with being a father than just having money. He didn't know anything about babies, but he could handle it one of two ways. He could take the sucka route and just give her money, or he could take the time to slow down and learn how to parent his child. Choosing the latter, Zoe walked over to Erica. The intensity on his face scared her some.

"I need you to chill with the crazy questions and comments. Everything will get shut down for my baby. You got that?"

With a broad smile on her face, Erica simply nodded. She wrapped her arms around Zoe's neck, and he held her tight. They were having a baby.

The city was on fire with the cops everywhere shaking down corner boys and pulling over every car with tinted windows. Gutta's face was still all over the news, and it had been like hell trying to get him out of the city for the past couple of hours. Everybody got close to $400,000 from the bank, and that wasn't even including some of the jewelry that was in the deposit boxes. Trust still couldn't figure out why Monica wanted the bank statements Gutta said he got out of deposit box B-6. But whatever she wanted with them, they were all hers.

Hearing his phone ring, Trust looked down at it and wondered who was calling him from a blocked number. If it was Monica, she was calling way past the time she said she would.

"Yo, who dis?" Trust answered in a low voice the way he did whenever someone called him from a blocked number.

"It's Monica."

"Why are you just now calling me?" Trust said with an attitude, hating that she wasn't on time.

I'm sorry. The Feds questioned me for hours, and I finally got free. I really didn't know if my phone was bugged either, so I didn't want to take the chance of hitting you up," Monica said, trying to be calm.

"So how do you know that your phone isn't tapped right now?" he replied.

"I'm not sure, but I had to call you to see if you can bring me what I asked for. Besides, I'm calling you from my sister's phone. I came here right after the Feds let me go."

"Yeah, I got ya cut, and the paperwork right here—"

"Paperwork?" Monica said, cutting Trust off. "I didn't tell you to get me no paperwork," she snapped back.

"What are you talking about? That's what was in B-6," Trust said, becoming confused about what Monica was looking for.

"I don't know what kind of games you're playing, but I want my diamonds."

"Diamonds?" he asked with a shocked look on his face.

"Yeah, diamonds. Twenty million dollars' worth. You must be a damn fool if you think I was doing all of this for some fuckin' paperwork. Somebody in ya crew is lying to you, so you better find out who it is and who got my diamonds before I send all of y'all asses to jail," Monica threatened, then hung up the phone.

Trust got up and looked around the house for Gutta, who now was just supposed to be waiting until the heat died down before they tried again to move him out of the city. All kinds of thoughts ran through Trust's mind, especially hearing that there was an extra $20 million involved.

"Where is Gutta?" Trust asked Zoe, who was sitting on the couch watching TV. Zoe had managed to get home, put his money up, and then come back to the spot with no problems.

"He went to go put his money up," Zoe told Trust.

"No, he didn't. Get up and grab your gun. He's tryin' to get out of town tonight."

"Why would he take that risk when the cops are still running around the city?"

"I got twenty million reasons why," Trust said. He loaded up his gun, and they headed out the door.

"Monica wasn't exactly honest with me, and Gutta isn't being honest with either of us. Monica just called me and asked me for her diamonds. Twenty million dollars' worth. Box B-6 had diamonds in it. That's why she only wanted what was in the box," he explained to Zoe as they got into the car.

The plan to get Gutta out of the city was to wait until it was late at night, find the last Greyhound bus leaving the station, and take that to wherever it was going. Once he got out of the city, he could freely take a bus to wherever he wanted to go without worrying about his face being all over the news. It was 11:00, and the last bus for Atlantic City was leaving at 12:45 a.m. The last thing Trust was about to do was let Gutta leave town with the diamonds before he could get part of it. Hell, for $20 million in diamonds, Gutta was liable to be found floating in the Delaware River by the end of the night. After all, Gutta was the one acting sheisty, sneaky, and slimy. If he had any loyalty to the crew who took him in and got him rich when he was bound to go to jail trying to make a buck, the last thing he would've done was stash extra money from the crew, especially when everybody was paid equally after every job.

***

"Can I get a one-way ticket to Atlantic City?" Gutta asked the cashier, looking up at the bus schedules and noticing a bus was about to pull out to Atlantic City in about twenty minutes. Gutta felt as though he made the right choice in cutting off his beard. It made a big difference, because the two police officers at the entrance of the bus station didn't even look at him coming in. The plan was working so far, and the taste of freedom was on the other side of the doors leading to the buses that were about to depart. With his book bag full of money strapped to his back and a pocketful of diamonds, Gutta walked out onto the platform where the buses were and got into the line with his ticket in hand.

Agent Bell sat at the far end of the platform with a newspaper in her hand as if she were reading it, but really she was just using it as a front to look at Gutta's picture inside of it. *I have been sitting at this station for the past few hours, and I've seen about five people coming through here who look just like Gutta, and every one of them checked out to be someone else,* Bell thought, sizing up a bald guy with a book bag on who had just come out to the platform for Atlantic City. Bell got up and moved a little closer to get a better look at the man she thought could be Gutta. If only she could see the left side of his neck to see if he had a tattoo, she could get a positive ID on him.

Gutta stood in line looking at one of the diamonds he pulled from his pocket, waiting for the bus driver to start loading the bus. He was so into the diamond that he didn't even see Agent Bell walk up behind him and stand in line like she was about to get on the bus.

Looking around to the left side of his neck, Bell almost had a heart attack, seeing the words "family first" on the side of his neck. It was Gutta, and Bell knew this for sure.

Chapter Ten

Bell pulled her gun from her holster and put it directly to the back of Gutta's head, grabbing a hold of the book bag in case he decided to run. She was more afraid of Gutta than he was of her, and the fact that she had seen the bodies of Gutta's victims didn't make it any easier for her.

"FBI. Don't move or I swear I'll shoot. Robert Green, you're under arrest for the murder . . ."

Hearing those words sent chills down Gutta's spine. Up until that moment, he thought he was scot-free. Gutta turned around to face Bell, not afraid of the gun that was now pointing in his face.

"I'll tell you what: if you let me go, I'll give you this," Gutta said, holding up the diamond he had in his hand. "I'm sure it's worth a lot of money." When Bell looked at the diamond, Gutta smacked the gun away, barely dodging the bullet that was fired from Bell's reaction. He punched her in the jaw with an overhand right hook, knocking her to the ground. He pulled out his gun from his waist and stood over her with it pointed at her head.

Several shots rang out, stopping Gutta from squeezing the trigger as he dipped off looking for cover behind the bus. Agent Bell managed to get to her feet. She fired several shots at Gutta but missed because her equilibrium was thrown off by the punch. The two police officers who were in the bus station walked through the broken glass from the doors of the bus station with their guns out, yelling for Bell to drop her weapon.

"I'm FBI! I'm FBI!" she yelled out, showing her badge hanging around her neck.

Zoe came from behind the building with his gun in hand only to be met by gunfire from both the police on the platform and by Gutta, who was behind the bus. Dipping back behind the wall, Zoe fired back, hitting one of the cops in the shoulder and knocking holes the size of golf balls into the bus.

The frantic patrons of the bus station all took cover. Gutta was behind the bus. Bell was behind a soda machine. Zoe was behind the wall. One cop was behind a cement trash can. The other cop attempted to run into the station for cover, but he was met by Trust, who shot him in the neck and upper chest before taking cover behind a vending machine.

"Gutta, you're going to jail!" Bell yelled out, her heart beating rapidly in her chest. "There's nowhere for you to go!"

"Jail? Bitch, you're going to hell as soon as you show your pretty little face around that soda machine," Gutta shot back, reloading his gun.

"Gutta, you tried to shoot me, you stupid muthafucka!" Zoe yelled out.

"Fuck you, Zoe. I know what you came here for. Where's ya daddy, Trust? I know he's here with you."

"I'ma kill you, Gutta!" Trust yelled from inside of the station.

"Come on, Trust, you would've done the same thing if you had seen the size of these rocks. I was going to call you after I got out of the city."

"You slimy nigga. We were supposed to be partners."

"Yeah, well, it's a little too late for that," Gutta said, firing two shots into the building.

The sounds of cop cars flooded the night coming in the direction of the bus station. Without another word,

Trust backed out of the bus station on his knees, tucking his gun in his waist so he could move faster. On his way out the door, he could see several police cars coming to a screeching halt in front of the building. To them, Trust just looked like a victim, and the shots being fired from inside made them walk over him like he wasn't even there.

Firing several shots in the direction of Agent Bell, Gutta climbed into the driver-side window of the bus and started the engine. That prompted both the agent and the officer behind the trash can to start shooting at the bus in an attempt to hit Gutta or disable the bus before he pulled off. Gutta fired back, pulling off from the station, sideswiping cars on his way out of the lot. Police officers who had just gotten to the scene joined the agent running beside the bus shooting into the windows. One of the officers shot out the two right rear tires, but it didn't stop Gutta from pulling into the street, hitting anything in his path.

The bus headed for the Ben Franklin Bridge, and the cop cars hadn't yet caught up to him, giving Gutta a little distance to work with as he went over the bridge. By the time the Philly cops got over the bridge, the bus had crashed into a wall at the first exit at the end of the bridge, six blocks from the federal courthouse. The bus was abandoned when the cops surrounded it, and there was no sign of Gutta anywhere. The book bag and diamonds weren't anywhere to be found. Helicopters flooded the sky, and cop cars combed the streets looking for Gutta. The cops thought he couldn't get very far in such little time.

"I want an eight-mile square perimeter blocked off and a police officer walking on every street," Agent Bell demanded from the local police and the Philadelphia police who had come across the bridge. "Look in every dumpster. Overturn every rock. Check every parked car. Search every abandoned house and detain anybody with a bald head until I clear them to leave," Bell said, walking down the street, pointing and directing the police.

Through all the commotion, Zoe was able to slip away from the scene and make it back to Trust's car at the same time Trust did. With all the police chasing Gutta, it was easy for them to fade into the night without anybody knowing they were even there, even though everybody except Agent Bell had heard Gutta yell out both Trust and Zoe's name during the shoot-out.

The area was blocked off and police were combing the streets. The manhunt for Gutta continued and would continue until he was caught. One cop, while checking the area by the bridge, noticed someone who he thought may have been a homeless person curled up between two beams at the end of the bridge. He noticed the man had a bald head, but he wasn't able to see his face. He turned around and called for backup, trying to do it in a manner that wouldn't tip the guy off that he knew he was there. Bell was the first person on the scene with her gun drawn. It was Gutta. Bell knew it but feared another shootout, so she fired a warning shot, hitting the dirt underneath the beam.

"Gutta, if that's you, I need you to show me your hands!" Bell yelled out, pointing her gun directly at the top of his head. "There are only two ways out of this, Gutta: in a body bag or in a pair of handcuffs. The choice is yours."

"I'm shot," Gutta managed to get out, slowly moving from between the beams. "Don't shoot! Don't shoot!" he yelled out. Surely if Gutta had any more bullets in his gun, he would have gone out in a blaze of glory before he went to jail. With a gunshot to his abdomen, all he wanted right now was some medical attention.

"Where's the book bag, Gutta?" Bell asked while the police officer handcuffed him. "I need to know what you did with the bag," she said, thinking that the diamonds were in the bag. Gutta didn't answer her, but he smiled as they put him into the back of the police car. Gutta knew exactly what she wanted and was glad he hid the diamonds before he got caught or got killed.

Getting into her car to follow Gutta being transported to the hospital, Bell pulled a diamond out of her pocket. Gutta had dropped one during the shoot-out. She sat in her car with the interior light on, mesmerized by the stone and its size. Knowing what a real diamond looked like, Bell's pussy started to get wet just looking at it. It was orgasmic, and the more she looked at it, she began to rub the wetness of her pussy through her pants with one hand while holding the diamond in the other. If it weren't for the other cops coming up to the car to check up on her, she would have sat there for a while longer to enjoy the cum that moistened her panties. Diamonds were truly her best friend.

Trust's phone wouldn't stop ringing, and he didn't want to answer it because it was Monica. After what she had said to Trust about sending him to jail, he thought about killing her before she got the chance to tell anything. He knew she wouldn't stop calling, however, and if she felt that he played her, she'd for sure drop his name to the police.

"What's up, Monica?" Trust answered the phone with an attitude as he drove down the highway.

"Hey, I'm sorry about what I said earlier when I said I was going to send you to jail. I just want the diamonds, so can you hurry up and get them to me?" Monica's voice was anxious.

"Yeah, well, I'm not trying to do too much talking over the phone. I can tell you one thing, those diamonds are long gone, and if you turn on the news, you'll know exactly what I'm talking about. Call me tomorrow so that we can talk face-to-face," Trust told Monica before hanging up in her ear.

As soon as he hung up the phone, it started ringing again. This time it was Faith, the one person he could never deny talking to. "Hey, beautiful," he answered with a smile on his face.

"Hey, mister, you coming to pick me up from work, or did you forget about me working late tonight?" Faith's voice was so sexy to Trust that sometimes he forgot what the conversation was about if she said more than ten words.

"No, baby, I didn't forget about you," Trust said, lying through his two front teeth. With everything that had gone on tonight, Faith would have ended up catching an Uber home if she hadn't called him. "I'm not too far from you now. Meet me outside in about ten minutes," he added before hanging up.

"That's not enough. I need you to get him to admit to the robbery," Agent Ralley demanded of Monica when she hung up the phone with Trust. "If you want the prosecutor to cut you some slack, you'd better get Trust talking, and you'd better get him talking quick, or you'll be going to jail by yourself."

Monica couldn't handle the interrogation after she met with the agent after the robbery, so she gave in. She was cooperating with the government in hopes of staying out of prison and still managing to get some of the diamonds in the process.

"I will wear a wire. Tomorrow when I meet with Trust, I will wear a wire, and I will get him to confess to the robbery," Monica said, sitting in her living room with a scared look on her face.

That's all Ralley wanted to hear as he pulled out his phone to call headquarters to take out the equipment. From the evidence at the bank, Ralley knew for sure that these were the guys he'd been looking for. He was more determined than ever to catch them, with the help of Monica, of course. This would be the big case he needed to retire from the force with, that and a couple million dollars' worth of diamonds after he found them, if he found them at all. He was going to go to great lengths to get some of that dirty money going around, even if that meant getting a little dirty himself.

Trust pulled up in front of the hospital. Faith came out with her light blue smock on with her hair sweated out like she'd had a rough night. Like the gentleman she'd made him become, Trust got out of the car and greeted her with a hug and a kiss before opening the door for her to get into the car. When Trust got into the car, Faith just looked at him with a smile on her face, but the smile quickly turned into a frown as Trust was pulling off.

"Baby, I need to talk to you about something very important, but first I need to know what's going on with you. What's going on in your life right now? And don't tell me nothing, because I know you better than you think I know you." Faith didn't feel anymore that she was just being paranoid about how Trust made his money. Something was for sure off about him. Either he was cheating or hiding something from her, or both, but she needed to know what was up.

"I don't know what to say, babe. I've just been really working hard, and I guess I'm kind of tired."

"Tired of what, Trust? Is it just mentally exhausting? I'm not downplaying what you do, but there's a lot of money and technicalities. It's not like you're the one at the store running the register or at the rental properties dealing with the tenants. So, tell me, babe, what's going on? I thought we agreed that we would always be truthful with one another no matter what. You know you can confide in me about anything."

"Yeah, I know. It's just that some things are best for you not to know about me for your own good. All you need to know is that I will never cheat on you and you're the only one for me. I love you beyond what your mind can ever comprehend, and it's you I want to spend the rest of my life with."

"You swear you mackin', nigga. Don't run that game on me," Faith said, smiling at how Trust chose his words. "You know, if you don't want to tell me, that's fine. When you get ready, and that'd better be soon, you'll tell me. When you do, you're going to see that it will never change how I feel about you."

"So, what was it you wanted to talk to me about, Ms. Lady?" Trust said, poking Faith in her side.

Faith looked nervous about telling Trust that she was pregnant. Now that she knew he was hiding something about his life, she didn't want to take the chance of making his life any more difficult with the news of a baby than what it was.

"What? What are you thinking about?" Trust asked, seeing Faith in a daze.

"Well, unlike you, I'm not going to hide anything about my life to you, because I love you enough to share my whole world with you."

"Yeah, yeah. Cut the game and spit it out, Faith."

"Trust, I'm pregnant."

Almost sideswiping a parked car, Trust swerved back into his lane. Inside the car was silence, and neither one of them even blinked for a moment until Faith broke the silence.

"Say something, Trust. What's going on in that thick-ass head of yours?" she said, poking him in his head. "Say something stupid," Faith said, now on the verge of tears at the thought of Trust not wanting the baby.

Trust pulled over and got out of the car, popping the trunk open as he exited the car. Faith didn't know what he was doing as he rummaged through the trunk. Now getting kind of scared, when Trust walked up to her door, she locked it so he couldn't get in. Trust couldn't do anything but smile at the thought of Faith locking the door out of fear. In his hand there was a box, and when he opened it, Faith's eyes got wide at the sight of a ring. She rolled the window down to get a better look at it, and that was when Trust got down on both of his knees.

"I've been waiting for this moment for a long time," Trust began. "To be with you, to raise a family with you, to share my soul with you, and to make you my wife. From this day forward, I want you to be the caretaker of my heart. I want you to be my wife, Faith. Will you please marry me, babe?" Trust said with so much sincerity that it gave her chills.

Faith had to take slow, steady breaths to keep herself from hyperventilating. A proposal from Trust certainly wasn't what she expected, but she was ecstatic. Tears spilled over her eyelids as a wide smile crossed her face. "Of course I'll marry you, baby." She got out of the car, and as soon as Trust stood up, she jumped into his arms.

For one brief moment, Trust was able to forget about all the chaos brewing in his life.

Chapter Eleven

Wanda watched the news with her mouth hanging open. As she stared at the picture of Gutta plastered on the screen, she listened to the reporter giving details of a shoot-out in the bus station. The events at the bus station supposedly stemmed from a bank robbery of some sort and a murder. Wanda was stunned. She knew Gutta was in the streets, but she had no idea he was doing all of that. He hadn't been home since the police hemmed her up, but in the back of her mind, Wanda always had hopes that Gutta would calm down and come back to her. She just wanted him to walk through those doors, sit down on the couch, and talk to her, but as she watched the news, she knew that wouldn't happen. *How can you live with a person and know so little about them?*

Wanda's phone rang, and her heart pounded fast in her chest. Each time her phone rang, she prayed it was Gutta. Her heart rate returned to its normal rhythm, and it sank a little when she saw that her mother was calling. She had no doubt seen the news and was calling to ask her daughter about Gutta. Wanda didn't feel like talking. Gutta wasn't just some bank robber or savage criminal to her. He was her lover. Her friend. They lived together. Now she was faced with the possibility that she may never see him as a free man again. Where in the hell would that leave her? Shit, would he even make it to prison? Once the reporter started talking about him getting shot, the floodgates opened, and Wanda began to cry. What in the hell had Gutta gotten himself into?

***

Agent Bell walked into the hospital room where Gutta was recovering from minor stomach surgery, and she cleared the room of police officers who were on watch. Pulling her gun from her holster, she stuck it into the bloodstained bandage on his stomach, painfully waking him up.

"You know, you're a hard man to catch up with, Mr. Green," she said as she made her way around the other side of the bed without removing the gun from his stomach. "For a moment, I didn't think you would make it out of this alive, and to be honest with you, I'm kind of disappointed. Now I have a few questions for you, and it will be in your best interest to tell me the truth."

Gutta lay in bed in pain from the gun that was still in his gut. He couldn't do anything because both of his hands were cuffed to the bed. To make things worse, nobody else was in the room, leaving Bell to do pretty much whatever she wanted to do.

"Tell me, Gutta, where does a lowlife like you have a chance to come across a diamond like this?" she said, playing with the diamond in her hand and removing the gun from his gut so that he could talk.

Gutta smiled through the pain of his injury, seeing the desire in Bell's eyes as she played with the diamond. "I was just getting ready to propose to my girlfriend with that diamond you got in ya hand. I got it from the gumball machine two days ago," Gutta joked. "I thought I was being investigated for murder, not fake diamonds. If you're going to charge me, then charge me. If not, get the fuck out of my room or stick that piece of shit gun back into my gut and end my misery." A sick grin covered his face.

"That's fine, Gutta. Have it your way. But know that eventually you're going to talk to me whether you like it or not. If not, then I'm sure I can make this a death penalty case, and you're going to have all kinds of medications going into your arms, killing you with your eyes wide open. Nothing to worry about for a gangsta like you," Bell said, walking toward the door. "I'll check back with you in a couple of days," were the last words that came from her mouth as she faded into the hallway and two uniform cops came back into the room.

It had been a couple of days since the shoot-out at the bus station, but the heat was still on in the streets. Both the police and the Feds were pretty much everywhere. For the most part, Trust had been spending a lot of time with Faith, now knowing that she was carrying his child. He was doing his best to show her that he was going to be a good father, but there were also a few things in his life that he had to wrap up before they came back to haunt him.

Trust's phone went off while he and Faith were sitting at the dining table eating lunch. Faith gave him a look that dared him to answer the phone while they were enjoying the moment. Not intending to answer it, he looked down at the phone out of curiosity to see who it was. It was none other than Monica. Being so caught up with Faith, he'd forgotten about the meeting they were supposed to have. This was one of the doors he had to close in his life, and he was ready to face it now more than ever. He had to take this call even though he didn't want to and despite the look he was getting from Faith.

"Yeah, what's good?" Trust answered, getting up from the table like he normally did when he had to take a call.

"Are you home?" a voice said into the phone. It didn't sound like Monica.

"Naw, I'm not home yet," Trust shot back, thinking fast on his feet. He walked over into the bedroom and looked out the window. Several cop cars pulled up in front of the condominiums, including a few unmarked cars. The person on the other end of the phone had hung up before he could ask who it was.

Faith came into the room, seeing that something was wrong, and watched Trust as he hurriedly began grabbing items off the dresser. "Trust, what's going on?" she asked, becoming worried.

"Babe, I don't have time to explain, but the cops will be in here in about one minute," he stated, turning his attention to Faith, who had sat down on the bed. "I promise that I will tell you about everything later. When they come in here, just tell them that I'm not here and you don't know anything about me," Trust instructed as he grabbed some money and a gun out of the closet.

"Get up," he urged her, and she did so with a confused expression on her face. Without warning, Trust lifted the bed, revealing a trapdoor he'd installed when they moved into the condo. Faith didn't even have an idea that the trapdoor was there, and she had been under the bed for numerous things in the past. The door was built into the floor, was covered by carpet, and had a small latch that wasn't visible to the naked eye. The space was only built for one person, and it led to the garbage shoot in the hallway.

"I love you, baby," he said, climbing into the space and motioning for Faith to drop the bed back down, which she did once his head was clear.

"FBI! FBI! Don't move!" Several agents yelled, coming through the front door after ramming it down. The loud sound of the bedroom door crashing open and the large machine guns pointing right in her face were enough to make Faith scream, but she held herself together and complied with the demands from the agents for her to get down on the ground.

I can't believe this bitch ratted us out, Trust thought, crawling on his stomach toward the garbage shoot. He could hear the footsteps of the agents right above him and them yelling at Faith to say where he was. "I knew I couldn't trust dis bitch," he mumbled to himself. "I should have killed dat bitch. Fuck, I gotta call Zoe before the police get to him."

Chapter Twelve

The quiet South Philly streets became flooded with federal cop cars pulling up to Zoe's house. Zoe could hear the tires come to a screeching halt, which woke him and Erica out of their sleep. He looked out the window and could see the U.S. Marshals taking the battering ram out of the trunk of one of their cars.

"We got a problem," Zoe said, jumping out of the bed and heading for the closet.

Erica jumped up too, not asking questions but following her man's suit. Zoe grabbed an M-16 from the closet, popped a fifty-round clip in it, and proceeded downstairs. Erica did the same thing, except she grabbed an AK-47 from under the mattress, clicking the switch over to fully automatic. She chose to stay upstairs. She had no clue what was going on, but she was riding for her man.

Before the battering ram could even touch the door, police could hear shots coming from inside the house. Zoe began firing at the front door with the M-16, and once Erica heard that, she began firing from the window, striking one of the agents before he got a chance to take cover. Marshals and agents ducked behind cars, trying to avoid the bullets that were coming from ground level and from above their heads. Bullets were just missing their heads, and the sound of the bullets hitting the cars sounded like the beginning of a piano solo.

Zoe threw a chair through the front window to get a better look at the Marshals as he continued to fire upon them with the M-16. The bullets ripped through the cars, knocking glass into the faces of the Marshals who found it hard to get out of the way of the hailing bullets. The Marshals didn't even have a chance to shoot back, because if Zoe wasn't hitting them from downstairs, Erica was keeping them at bay from upstairs.

"Let's go!" Zoe screamed upstairs for Erica to come downstairs, which she did as quickly as she could. "Head for the back door," he instructed. "I'm right behind you," he said, tapping her on her ass.

Erica headed for the back door, popping the clip out of the AK-47 and turning it upside down to a fresh clip. Zoe was right behind her, but after a break from the bullets flying out of the house, the Marshals and the agents began firing into the house, round after round, clip after clip. The bullets knocked chips of wood and sheetrock all over Zoe and Erica as they headed down the hallway toward the back door.

Stopped at the back door by gunfire from a single Marshal in the back alleyway, Erica fired several shots in his direction, hitting him in the neck and head, killing him instantly. The other Marshals were unsure of where Zoe and Erica were, so they slowly crept up to the house, providing more than enough time for Zoe and Erica to slip out the back door and into the backyard of the neighbor's house directly across the alleyway. It was only by God's grace that Zoe was able to kick in the front door. The neighbors, who had been awakened by the gunfire, stood in awe as Zoe and Erica ran through their house and out the back door. It was some shit straight out of a movie. On the street, Erica stopped the first oncoming car, raising the AK-47, forcing the driver to stop and get out of the car. Before the Feds even got through the house, they had already made a speedy getaway with Zoe behind the wheel.

Left behind was a dead Marshal, a shot agent, and a house full of bullet holes. The Feds never knew what hit them. Only one car was operable, and it was blocked in by the other cars that had flat tires and busted engines from the large-caliber bullets that had torn through them. The modern-day Bonnie and Clyde had flooded the streets of South Philly with massive gunfire, disrupting the beautiful Thursday afternoon.

Monica mentioned only the names of Trust, Zoe, and Gutta because they were the only ones she met. For the time being, Amy wasn't under any investigation and was able to go about her daily life with close to half a million dollars in her possession. She made a few upgrades to the club like new barstools and new office decor, and she even thought about turning the basement into a XXX-rated lounge where there would be all-nude dancers who would fuck for a buck and do some "strange thangs" for some change.

Amy looked down at her phone and was pleased that it was Trust calling her. She hadn't heard much from him since the robbery. "Hey, handsome," she answered with a big smile on her face.

"Come to your back door," Trust said quietly into the phone before hanging up.

Amy went to the back door, clutching a blue steel .357 revolver, not liking the tone of Trust's voice. When she got to the door and opened it, Trust was sitting beside the club's dumpster as if he were hiding from somebody. His clothes looked dusty, and his shirt even had a rip in it.

Trust quickly walked into the club but not before looking up and down the alleyway two or three times, trying to make sure he wasn't being followed by the Feds.

"Trust, what the hell is going on?" Amy asked as she locked the door, still clutching her gun.

"The Feds just raided my spot. Da bitch Monica is a rat now. Things got real ugly the past few nights, and Gutta got locked up, too," he explained, walking behind the bar and grabbing a bottle of vodka. "You know the deposit box we were supposed to get for Monica? It had twenty million dollars' worth of diamonds in it, and Gutta kept them for himself," Trust said, taking a swig from the bottle.

"Twenty million?" she asked in shock.

"Yeah, twenty million in ice. He's locked up in the county jail for the time being, and the Feds will be there any minute to holla at him if they haven't already."

Amy just stood there with her mouth wide open as Trust broke down everything that was going on with Gutta and the diamonds. He could see the confusion in her face. She'd thought that Gutta was a part of the family Trust built. But in all actuality, he was proving to be a snake. She too had watched as Trust made Gutta rich after he was just a petty thief. Gutta always talked about how loyal he was to the crew, and no matter what he did on his own time, the crew could always depend on him when it mattered. *All that was a bunch of lies,* Amy thought, grabbing a white T-shirt from under the counter to give to Trust.

"Does he still have the diamonds?" Amy asked out of curiosity.

"If I know Gutta the way I think I do, he stashed those diamonds before the cops got to him. If he didn't, then he's pretty much fucked for those murders in the projects. Look, Monica never met you, so you're cool. The Feds aren't looking for you. I need you to go visit Gutta before the Feds take him into custody."

Trust stopped talking and focused on the TV that was sitting at the corner of the bar. He couldn't believe his eyes as he walked closer to the TV, seeing Zoe's face covering the whole screen, followed by a picture of himself and Gutta. Trust's heart dropped, and he had to sit down in a chair before he passed out. The news anchor talked about how they were wanted for the bank robbery that took place in Center City and about the murders Gutta was locked up for. One U.S. Marshal was dead, and a federal agent was critically wounded due to the attempted arrest on Zoe earlier that day at his house. Zoe and his unidentified female accomplice had fled the scene after a seven-minute shoot-out with authorities.

Just then, Trust's phone started to ring, breaking his trance from the TV. Although the phone number was blocked, something told him to answer it. "Yo," Trust said into the phone, looking back up at the TV.

"You see the news?" a weak voice said into the phone.

"Yeah, I'm looking at it right now. I thought this might be you calling," Trust said, happy to hear from Zoe. "Are you okay?"

"I'm good. Look, old head, I didn't have any other choice, and I told you that I will never be willing to go to jail, under no circumstances—"

"I'm not mad at you. I'm just glad to hear from you," Trust said, cutting him off. "Look, we got to meet up. Don't tell me where you are over this phone. Just listen to me. Remember back in the day when those two guys tried to rob me, and you stood up for me? Meet me at the place I was on my way to before it happened. You got me?"

"I remember."

"Do you still have money?"

"Yeah. They didn't get any of that," Zoe said, relieved that he kept his money in a separate place from where he lived.

"All right, meet me in two hours. The sun should be going down by then. Oh, and don't call this phone ever again. I'll have a new number for you when I see you," Trust said, hanging up the phone and throwing it into a sink full of soapy water Amy was using to clean dishes.

"So, what now?" Amy asked, looking at the concern in Trust's eyes.

"I got a big mess to clean up, but first I got to get Zoe and Faith out of the city and as far away as possible. I need you to go holla at Gutta in the morning. I'll call you tonight with my new number."

"Trust, be careful, please. If you need me, you better call me. C'mere," she said, choking back tears and pulling him by his arm, leading him to the storage room. "Take a couple of these with you. I stocked up on these for situations like this," Amy said, opening up a deep freezer, pushing beers to the side, and exposing several semiautomatic handguns with extra clips. "And you're definitely going to need this," she said, tossing him a bulletproof vest.

Trust looked so stressed out. He had so much on his mind, and he didn't even know where to start. It was a must that he find Monica and kill her before she put everybody in jail for a long time. But before he did anything, he had to find a way to get Zoe, his girlfriend, and Faith out of the city, all while trying to get the diamonds from Gutta, who was sitting in the county jail with detectives and FBI agents up his ass around the clock. It was a lot to handle, but Trust had no other choice.

Chapter Thirteen

Faith rocked back and forth slowly with one hand clutching her flat belly and the other covering her mouth. Deep, gut-wrenching sobs left her mouth as she watched the news. *Trust is a fucking bank robber? How? Why? That's how he's been able to afford to spoil me?* Barbie had been right. He was doing other shit. Faith didn't even have time to be angry at him. She was worried beyond belief, so worried that it was making her physically ill. Faith gagged and hopped up off the bed in just enough time to make it to the master bathroom and throw her guts up. The Feds had questioned her for hours. By the time they were satisfied that she didn't know shit and let her go, she was exhausted, but sleep refused to find her. Why would Trust keep all of this from her? And now she was pregnant. Crying was all Faith could do.

Just the thought of Barbie and her parents getting a hold of this information was enough to make her groan. Her coworkers knew Trust. How was she supposed to show her face at work? Faith didn't know when she would hear from Trust again, and that made her livid. *This is why he shouldn't keep secrets.* After she flushed the toilet, Faith brushed her teeth, and as she stared at her reflection in the mirror, she caught a glimpse of her engagement ring. There would be no wedding. There would be no happily ever after. Her entire relationship had been a lie. It had all been one big, fat-ass lie. How could Trust do that to her?

Once Faith was done brushing her teeth, she took her clothes off and got in the shower. She felt physically weak, and all she wanted to do was get into bed and curl up into a ball. If it were up to her, she'd never show her face in public again. Life as she knew it was over.

"Green, you have a visitor!" the guard yelled out into the housing unit where Gutta was sitting at a table playing Spades.

It took Gutta fifteen minutes to get to the visiting room, which was only a three-minute walk from the pod. A lot of stopping and talking to some of his homies he knew from the streets was what took up time. The bullet wound to his stomach was beginning to heal, but he was still unable to move as swiftly as he could before. He felt that the officers at the prison had it in for him because they refused to give him the good shit. The fact that he was in pain should have been obvious, but they would give him Motrin whenever he complained. It was cool, because they didn't know Gutta was a certified G. He took that shit like a champ.

Thinking that it was probably Wanda coming to see him, it was a surprise to walk into the visiting room and see Agent Bell waiting for him. It was even more confusing to Gutta because she was in the social visiting room instead of the legal booth, where attorneys usually visited their clients.

Hesitant but curious, Gutta took a seat right in front of Bell. "What can I do for you?" he asked with a smirk on his face while he took the time to take in Agent Bell's face.

She looked very different that day. In fact, she didn't look like a federal agent at all. From the moment he'd laid eyes on her, even in strenuous conditions, Gutta could see that Bell was gorgeous. She appeared to be a mix of something, but he didn't know what. She was a very pretty woman with skin the color of heavily creamed coffee, and her hair was long, blond, and curly. She had on a light blue fitted T-shirt that showed off her belly button, a pair of True Religion hip-hugger jeans, and a pair of black peep-toe heels by Steve Madden. Her breasts were a 36-D cup, and you could tell that she didn't need a bra to hold them up because of their firmness. She was the baddest piece in the visiting room, hands down.

"How are you doing, Gutta?" she said, smiling as though she was happy to see him. "I see you got yourself a haircut. Were you expecting somebody else to come see you today?"

"What did you come here for, Bell? I thought I already told you that I'm not working with the Feds or any other law enforcement agencies. So why don't you stop wasting your time barking up the wrong tree before that tree falls on you?"

Bell smiled. "You look cute when you get all gangsta like that. But you and I both know that no one is tough enough to want to spend the best years of their life on death row. I'ma cut to the chase and tell you the reason I'm here. About a week ago a bank was robbed downtown, and among the things that were taken were some diamonds. Twenty million dollars' worth, Gutta."

Trying to keep a straight face and maintain his composure, Gutta looked down to the ground like he wanted to tie his shoe. He was surprised at how much the diamonds were worth. Up until now, he didn't have the slightest idea that he was walking around with $20 million. It was at this point that Gutta started to feel like he was getting the upper hand.

"So, I guess you want to know where the diamonds are at," Gutta said, trying to keep his cool but also noticing how sexy Bell looked as a civilian. Her thighs were thick, and you could see her pussy print through her jeans as she leaned up to the edge of the chair.

"I have something you want, and you have something I want," Bell said, now sitting about a foot away from Gutta.

"What could you possibly have that I want?" Gutta shot back.

"I have your freedom."

"Agent Bell, if you haven't noticed, I'm in here for a triple homicide, drug trafficking, a shoot-out with you, and a possible bank robbery. I'm not sure that there's anything you can do for me at this point, and even if you thought you could, it would be hard to convince me."

Bell sat back in her chair to get all her thoughts together before she said what it was she was thinking. She could see her whole career as a Fed going down the drain if she made this deal with Gutta. But for $20 million in diamonds, she thought about all the new career choices that would be available for her as long as she didn't go to jail first.

"Well, as I see it, the only evidence we had on you for the drug trafficking crime was killed in the projects, and the only witness to that murder is a seventeen-year-old girl who identified you as the shooter. Without the girl we have no case at all, and she's sitting in protective custody right now in a safe house only a few other agents and I know about."

"Yeah, so what are you saying? You're going to eliminate that problem for me?" Gutta asked with an unbelievable look on his face.

"Let's put it like this, the next time your court hearing comes around, which would be next month, you might be walking out of here a free man."

"What about the shoot-out at the bus station?" Gutta asked, trying to cover all angles of possible prosecution.

"Well, you know, an officer was killed—"

"I didn't have anything to do with that," Gutta declared, cutting her off before she could say another word. "I was outside shooting at you when he got shot."

"Yeah, I know. The guy you were yelling at named Trust, that's his beef. As far as you shooting at me, stealing a bus, and going on a high-speed chase into another state, if you cooperate against Trust for the murder of the cop at the bus station, I'm sure my boss will negotiate a nice deal for you that would let you back out into the streets. Worst-case scenario, you might have to do a little time in jail, but nowhere close to the death penalty you're facing now."

"What about the bank robbery?"

"We'll cross that bridge when we get to it. I know for sure that it's not as bad as you think it is. No matter what the crime is, the Feds can always get someone out. We have the power to do anything."

Gutta just sat there listening to Bell, not knowing if he could trust her. He was also trying his best not to be hypnotized by how good Bell looked and the possibility of him getting closer to her in the near future.

"So, what you want, Bell? And don't play no games." He was indeed curious as to what Bell had in store.

Sitting up on the edge of her chair once again, but this time coming even closer to him, she put her hand on his lap. "I figure you and I could split the diamonds. Well, I get fifteen million and you get five because I'm putting more on the line than you. I could end up in jail right along with you if my plan doesn't work out. You just have to give me some time to find a buyer for the diamonds, and by this time next year, we could be in a foreign country, living like royalty."

Gutta caught on real fast to what Bell said. "What do you mean 'we' could be in a foreign country?"

"I didn't mean 'we' as in being together." She smirked. "I just meant that we wouldn't want to still be in the States if it's possible for us to pull this off. We wouldn't want to arouse any kind of suspicion."

"Why the fuck should I trust you? For all I know, you could be trying to set me up right now, *Agent* Bell," Gutta said, reminding her of who she was.

Bell grabbed Gutta's hand while still sitting on the edge of the chair. She raised his hand to her face, stuck his middle finger in her mouth, and sucked on it one time as though it were a dick, looking him in his eyes the whole time. Her mouth was warm and wet, and the sensation it gave Gutta made his mind wander. She then guided his hand down across her breast and then planted it directly onto her pussy through her pants. Gutta's dick was rock hard at this point, and the want to fuck Bell clouded his better judgment.

Angela had always been one of the good ones. She was even low-key surprised at how quickly she'd turned, but for $20 million in diamonds, her judgment was for sure clouded. She'd never get that kind of chance again, and she for damn sure wouldn't get rich chasing criminals like Gutta for years to come. Shit, she had done enough good. Angela felt as though she deserved a li'l come-up, and as she flirted with Gutta, she had to admit that thoughts of him fucking her savagely from the back made her pussy throb. She was tired of being the good girl who never came out on top, and she was damn sure tired of using a fuckin' vibrator four times a week.

"I didn't come here as an agent today, Gutta, and I'm probably not going to leave here as one. But rest assured I'm your only chance at seeing the streets again, so you just have to take my word. If this is any consolation, I'm a fool for diamonds," Bell said, getting up from her chair. "Think about it. And when you think about it, I want you to ask yourself if twenty million dollars is worth your freedom. It would be pretty hard to spend that kind of money from jail and not enjoy the fruits of it. Just think about it," Bell said before walking away toward the door where the guard was standing.

Gutta's dick was still hard watching Bell walk away, looking at her fat ass switching from side to side. He didn't know what to do as he remained planted in the chair trying to process what had just gone on. All he could think about was the warmth of her mouth wrapped around his finger, wondering how her lips would feel on his dick. He thought about her soft breast and the moistness between her legs as he felt the thickness of her pussy through her jeans, smelling his fingers to see if he could still smell her. At one point, she made him forget all about the diamonds or what they were worth and all that she offered to do for him. The fact that she would go to great lengths for the diamonds was not a surprise to Gutta. Most FBI agents were dirty behind the scenes, he imagined. They just took their picks of who they were going to be dirty with and how long they were going to be dirty for.

Being snapped out of his trance by the correctional officer, Gutta got up and headed back to his pod with more than enough to think about for the next couple of days until Bell would most likely return.

Chapter Fourteen

When Faith got a letter in the mail that had no return address, her heart beat profusely in her chest. It had only been two days since the last time she saw Trust, and she prayed to God that he had somehow slipped the letter in to her. With shaky hands she opened the letter, and a sense of relief washed over her when she saw one simple thing. It was an address. She knew that more than likely she was being watched. Faith would have to ensure that, as she drove to meet Trust, no one was following her. Her eyes were almost swollen shut from crying, and she was delirious with worry. No matter how upset she was with Trust, however, just the thought of seeing him was enough to bring a slight smile to her face.

Faith had barely been eating. She had called into work, and she hadn't even showered. Every second of every day her mind was consumed with thoughts of Trust. She still hadn't had the courage to talk to her family or friends. Faith was hiding out from the world. She was afraid and alone, and for as mad as she wanted to be at Trust, all she really cared about was him being okay. If he was telling her to meet him at a secret location, then that had to mean he was okay.

Faith hopped in the shower and cleaned her body as quickly as she could. Once her body was dry and she had put lotion on, she dressed comfortably in a white-and-black sweat suit and white sneakers. After pulling her hair back into a ponytail, Faith was ready to go. She grabbed her purse and snatched her keys off the dresser. Inside her car, Faith looked in her rearview mirror as she pulled off. She glanced in the mirror every few minutes at first in the car. When she was sure that no one was following her, Faith put the address from the note in the GPS system, and she saw that Trust was almost an hour away from her. She settled in for the long ride, continuing to glance in the mirror every so often. As badly as she wanted to see Trust and know that he was okay, she'd be damned if she led the police right to him. She was much smarter than that.

When her GPS alerted her that she only had ten miles until she reached her destination, it felt as if someone were doing backflips inside Faith's belly. She was nervous, and the physical effects of that were overwhelming. Her heart began to race, and a blanket of sweat decorated her forehead. Faith loved Trust more than anything. She wasn't quite sure why he chose the route of robbing banks. It was selfish, and it was dangerous, but she loved him, and not going to him wasn't an option.

Faith made sure to do the speed limit because she didn't want to risk getting pulled over, but she was more than anxious to get to Trust. When she pulled onto a residential street in a nice neighborhood, Faith breathed a sigh of relief. She was only a half mile away from her man, and he was safe. Excitement engulfed her, and Faith suddenly got an epiphany. She wasn't sure how the Feds worked, but she wasn't taking any chances. She hadn't been followed, but what if they were tracking her phone or her car? Faith turned her cell phone off and parked a street over from the address that she was given.

Once she got out of her car, it took every ounce of self-restraint that she had not to break out into a full-blown run. By the time she stepped up on the porch and knocked on the door, it felt as if her knees were going to give out on her. Faith licked her dry lips and waited for the door to be opened.

When she heard locks being turned, her breath caught in her throat. Then she locked eyes with Trust.

Faith erupted into tears standing right there on the porch. Trust opened the screen door and pulled Faith into his arms. While inhaling his scent, she cried into his chest. She was just grateful for the chance to be in his arms once again. Trust pulled Faith inside the house and closed the door behind him.

Faith backed out of Trust's embrace, wiped her tears, and observed her surroundings. The house was sparsely furnished, but it was nice and clean. The items that were inside were nice enough to give the place a homey feel. Faith was starting to feel like she didn't know her man at all.

"Where are we?" Her eyes connected with his, and Trust didn't miss the pain in her gaze.

"I got this spot about a year ago. Got an aunt who was visiting from Colorado to put it in her name. I only come out here twice a month to dust the furniture, check on things, relax my mind. I know I fucked up, Faith. I did a lot of fucked-up shit, but me keeping you in the dark was my way of protecting you. I was okay with leaving you to be questioned because I know they can't charge you with shit."

Faith let out an exasperated sigh. "Robbing banks though, Trust? I mean, really. Why? What if you get caught? Then what? I'm pregnant." Tears glistened in her eyes as she placed her hand on her flat tummy.

"Babe, I know it's hard to even comprehend all this, but if you don't do anything else, just believe in yo' nigga. I'm gonna always be good. I can't say the tough times won't come, but we're going to come out on top. Believe that." Trust spoke with conviction. His eyes bore into hers, and he really looked as if he believed what he was saying.

He was a very smart man. He'd never let her down before, and Faith loved him and believed in him, but it was still hard for her to feel okay. Trust sensed her apprehension, and he pulled Faith into his arms and hugged her tight.

"I know we have a lot to discuss. Shit is hectic, and I have a lot on my plate right now, but it's going to be okay," he whispered before placing a kiss on her forehead.

Faith hoped to God that he was right.

Hours later, Trust and Faith pulled up into the projects where he told Zoe to meet him. Trust was in one car, and Faith was in another. It was dark, but Trust could see Zoe and Erica sitting on a pair of steps on the side of one of the buildings. After pulling into the lot, Trust got out of the car and embraced Zoe with a thug hug, happy to see him alive but pressed to get him and Erica, along with Faith, out of the city. He acknowledged Erica, too, giving her props for having Zoe's back in such a crazy way.

"I got to get y'all out of the city tonight," Trust began. "They got our pictures all over the news on every station, and we're considered armed and dangerous, so if they see us, there won't be too much talking. I gave Faith the whip that I had stashed at my 'lie dead' crib. It was too risky for her to get a rental in her name. I've never driven the car before, so it will be good. She's going to drive y'all out of here. I was thinking about Atlanta or maybe even Florida for an extended vacation for all of you."

"What about you?" Zoe butted in. "You say it like you're not coming with us or something. If you don't go, I don't go. We in this together."

Trust grabbed the back of Zoe's neck and pulled him closer to him. "I can't have you in the city right now, young buck. I need somebody to look after Faith until I clean up the mess we made. I'm about to burn this city to the ground, and I don't want you getting caught up in the fire. You know I love you like we come from the same womb, and I'd be damned if I let something happen to you."

Trust gave Zoe a new cell phone. "I'll call you if I need you," Trust said, opening the car door and putting Zoe in the back seat, followed by Erica. "Call me when you get to Georgia, and be careful," he told Faith and then kissed her before she pulled off.

Trust had a lot of love for Zoe but thought that he would do a lot more damage if he did it alone. The thought of Faith and his baby being so far away from home for a long time played a part in why Trust wanted Zoe to leave. He wouldn't trust anybody else in the world to look after her but the one person he knew best, and Zoe was that person. He knew Zoe would be against leaving him, but Trust didn't care. He called the shots.

"Green, you have a visitor!" the guard yelled out to the pod.

Damn, I hope this ain't Bell coming back so soon. She said she'll be back in a couple days, and that was yesterday, Gutta thought on his way to the visiting room. It was a surprise but a relief to see that it was Amy and not Bell. But what was she doing there? Gutta kept a blank expression on his face as he sat down.

"What's up, Gutta?" she said as she watched him sit down in front of her. Amy was wearing a sweat suit and a pair of Air Force One sneakers with her hair in a ponytail.

"Who sent you? Trust? That's the only reason you would come see me, 'cause it damn sure ain't because you wanted to see how I was doing."

"You're right, Trust did send me, but I did want to see how you were doing. Even though you gave us your ass to kiss, you're still family, and family has always got to check up on one another."

"I wasn't family when Trust tried to kill me the other night, or when Zoe took a shot at me. I wasn't family then, was I?" Gutta shot back at her.

"You took twenty million dollars' worth of diamonds and didn't bother to tell anyone, and then you even attempted to skip town with them. We were supposed to be your family, and that's how you were gonna treat us? Hell yeah, Trust was mad, and if I had been there, I would have shot at you too. You got to look at all the jobs y'all been on and the relationship we all built behind them. Put the shoe on the other foot. How would you feel?"

Amy was talking down to Gutta, but at the same time she was making a lot of sense, and Gutta couldn't do anything but feel guilty about how slimy he was being to some good people. It had bothered him ever since the day he got the diamonds, because deep down inside he wanted to tell everybody about the fortune that he possessed, but his greedy side kept him from doing so. It's a fact about the old saying that "the truth hurts," because it did, and Gutta was hurting at the moment.

"So, I guess Trust wants the diamonds too?" Gutta asked with his head down.

"No. Trust didn't tell me to ask about the diamonds. He just told me to check up on you and to let you know that he got you a lawyer yesterday. The lawyer should be coming to see you in a couple of days," Amy lied, saying all the right things to soften up his heart. "He's out there right now trying to clean up the mess you made to avoid all of us going to jail."

"You're telling me that Trust doesn't want the diamonds?" Gutta asked, shocked. Trust was good people, but even that sounded too good to be true.

"Trust couldn't care less about those diamonds. Sometimes a friendship is worth more than money. If you don't call that family, then what is? He put five grand on your books so you can fall back and eat good, because he knows Wanda skipped town with whatever money you did have."

Thinking Wanda was out there busy making moves for him, Gutta never thought anything about her not coming to visit him much or hardly answering the phone when he called. It all made sense, and what was even crazier was that Trust was still trying to reach out to him after everything that had gone on. He was feeling the love from his crew, something that he didn't expect. After hearing Amy talking about the love, honor, and loyalty the crew was supposed to have for one another, it had Gutta damn near on the verge of tears, but he was too G to ever cry in jail even if he was away from the inmates.

"You know we can all make it out of this scot-free and with the diamonds," Gutta informed Amy.

"What do you mean, Gutta?" she asked, eager to hear what Gutta had to say and also to see if her plan was starting to take effect.

"I still have the diamonds, all twenty million dollars' worth. All the Feds got on me is a witness from the projects who said she saw the murder. That's the main case I got right now, and if somebody could make it so she can't testify, I think I could bargain my way out of the shoot-out case with my cut of the diamonds."

"What do you mean, your cut?"

"We can split the diamonds four ways among me, you, Trust and Zoe. But I need your word that y'all will get me out of here. I think five million apiece should be more than enough to get me out. Do you think that the crew could ever forgive me for the past if I can make things better for the future?" Gutta asked, hoping to get Amy's approval.

"This is what I'm going to do. When I leave here, I'm going to call Trust and let him know everything you just told me, and I'ma find out what he wants to do. Call my cell phone tonight, and I'll let you know what he said. I'm sure he's not going to have a problem with it, but he's going to want to talk to you before he does anything."

Amy got the rest of the details from Gutta concerning the witness and the FBI agent who claimed she was trying to help him out. He even told her where half the diamonds were in good faith, just to show how serious he was. The other half he kept for insurance.

So far, Amy's tactics were working, but at the same time she was starting to feel a little sorry for Gutta, seeing the sorrow and conviction in his speech. His previous actions told her that he didn't care about the whole family, love, and loyalty thing, but maybe he really was trying to make it right. Amy knew she had mad love for him because deep down inside she wanted to do anything to help Gutta, despite what he did. She would be willing to help him just as long as it didn't put her in jail with him. And her getting some of the diamonds would be an added incentive. As long as Gutta wasn't talking out his ass and giving her false hope.

As Amy was leaving the jail, Agent Ralley was entering it, and Gutta didn't even get a chance to make it back to the housing area before the guard yelled out his name again for a legal visit. Gutta thought that it might have been the lawyer Amy was talking about, but when he got to the room, he was met by the flashing of an FBI badge.

"What the hell do you want?" Gutta said, not even taking a seat in the chair in front of him.

Agent Ralley began pulling out photos from his folder and throwing them onto the table. The pictures were from the bank robbery in Center City, depicting four masked gunmen taking over the bank. Then Agent Ralley threw the picture of the deposit box B-6 from inside of the vault.

"What the hell is this supposed to mean?" Gutta asked, looking down at the pictures.

"See, son, you and ya boys got yourselves into a heap of shit. I've got somebody who can place you at the scene with Trust and Zoe and whoever else y'all had with you. I don't know who the other guy was, but eventually I'll catch him too," Ralley said while looking at Gutta like he was the scum of the earth. "Now there are only two things you can do. One, you cooperate with the government and testify against your crew for a time reduction, or two, you can spend the rest of your life in prison while your boys continue living their lives. That's not to mention the fact that I'm going to need the diamonds y'all took from the vault as well as the money that—"

"I want to see my lawyer," Gutta requested, cutting Ralley off in the middle of his speech.

"A lawyer ain't gonna do you any good, son. I'm trying to give you a way out," Ralley said, now getting frustrated at Gutta's refusal to cooperate. "If you give me the diamonds—"

"I thought I asked to speak with my lawyer," Gutta said, walking toward the door and then leaving the room.

Ralley stormed out of the visiting room knowing that with Monica alone and no other evidence, it wouldn't be an open-and-shut case. He needed more, and the one person who could lead him to a guilty verdict was on his way back to his cell, unwilling to cooperate. That was enough to drive any federal agent crazy.

As soon as Amy left the jail, the first person she called was Trust to explain everything Gutta had told her and where they could find half the diamonds. At first, Trust

couldn't care less about what happened to Gutta, but after hearing the conversation that had gone on between
him and Amy, the laws of loyalty began to set in. One
thing about Trust was that he was always true to his
word when he said he would do something, and by telling Gutta a long time ago that he wouldn't see anything
bad happen to him, he stood by his word and decided to
help him out, even though Gutta had stabbed him in the
back. He also took into consideration the $10 million in
diamonds Gutta was giving up in good faith. Trust could
easily take those diamonds and disappear, leaving Gutta
high and dry, but it would leave a blemish on his charac-
ter. That was something Trust couldn't live with.

Chapter Fifteen

Sitting in his car about three blocks from where Monica lived, Trust monitored her house for several hours only to find that she had been placed in an in-house witness protection program with a twenty-four-hour police watch. She was officially a federal witness and chose to cooperate with the law in exchange for not being thrown in jail. Two FBI agents sat in front of her house at all times. Even when the shift change occurred, nobody would leave their post until the relief showed up. Being that Monica didn't have a job anymore, she was always in the house unless she had very important errands to run. It didn't matter much to Trust that the Feds were watching her. All that mattered was that she had to be silenced, permanently.

Trust checked his gun to make sure that he had a bullet in the chamber. He screwed the silencer on tight before he got out of the car and faded into the night, using the neighboring backyards as a cover to reach Monica's house. In this neighborhood, the houses were pretty large, and the space between them was about the length of twenty-five feet, not including the driveway space. Trust had a lot of room to make it up and down the back way without being noticed by anyone. Noticing an agent making his way around the house, Trust slid between two houses just a few doors from Monica's house. The agent made his way around the premises and back into his car with the other agent, who was asleep on the driver's side.

Inside the house, Monica and her husband, Michael, were in the bedroom discussing separation and what he would leave her with in the event that they got a divorce. The conversation was heating up, and Monica began yelling at the sound of Michael's cell phone ringing, guessing that it was probably the other woman he was seeing. He walked out of the bedroom and headed downstairs with the phone so that he could answer it without the person on the other end catching an earful of Monica yelling.

As he made his way to the kitchen, he turned on the light because it was pitch-black downstairs except for the streetlights shining through the living room window blinds. Without warning, he was met by Trust coming from behind the refrigerator with his gun pointed directly in Michael's face. Michael damn near shit on himself.

Trust squeezed the trigger with no hesitation. The first bullet hit Mike right between the eyes, knocking his head backward as he fell to his knees, then face-first to the ground. All you could hear was the voice of the woman yelling on the other end of his cell phone still clutched in Mike's hand.

"Hello! Hello!" she yelled before hanging up, thinking that she must have lost the signal. It had been impossible for her to hear the shot, because the sound of it was like a spitball being shot out of a straw. Monica, who was upstairs, didn't even hear the shot.

Trust stepped over Mike's body, and before making his way upstairs, he fired two more shots into the back of his head for good measure.

Going up the steps, he could hear Monica in the bedroom talking to herself while trying to pack some clothes in a suitcase as if she were about to leave. "You ain't shit, Michael. You can have everything," Monica yelled as Trust walked into the room. "This marriage has been over, and it was dumb of me to even stay here for this long!"

Sensing movement out of the corner of her eye, Monica whirled around to continue chastising who she thought was Michael. She got the shock of her life and damn near had a heart attack at the sight of Trust clutching a chrome .45 automatic. She wanted to piss on herself, and her heart felt like it was about to explode through her chest.

"Trust? How did you get into my house? And where's Michael?"

Trust walked over to the dresser and sat on it, waving his gun at Monica, gesturing for her to sit on the bed. The look in his eyes was blank, and Monica didn't know whether to scream, beg for her life, or take off running.

"What did you tell the Feds?" Trust asked, now pointing the gun at Monica as she sat down on the bed crying.

She could barely get a word out as the tears rolled down her face. The swelling of her throat from fear made it hard for her to swallow. She knew that if she told Trust what she'd told the Feds, it would guarantee a death sentence, and she couldn't help but think about what Trust probably had done to Michael.

"I told them everything, Trust. They were going to put me in jail. You told me that nobody was going to get hurt, and then you went and shot the teller. What was I supposed to do?" she pleaded.

"You were supposed to keep your mouth shut and ask for a lawyer. Now you got the Feds kicking down our doors like we're the most wanted men in America. Then you had the audacity to tell me about some fucking diamonds after the robbery. I guess you were planning on leaving the country with twenty million dollars without cutting me in after my team took all the risks. Fuck you!" Trust said, walking up to Monica with the gun pointed at her chest.

Before she could get out a full scream, three bullets pierced her body, knocking her back onto the bed. Trust stood over her and fired two more shots into her neck and face.

With his gun still in his hand, Trust calmly walked out of the room and down the stairs, out through the back door, and was met by one of the federal agents doing his rounds. It was too late for Trust to do anything other than what he did in this situation. He raised his gun and fired two shots into the agent's head, killing him instantly before he got the chance to pull the gun from his holster.

Damn! Trust had not wanted to but was forced to shoot the agent. He dragged the agent's lifeless body into the house and laid him right next to Michael. Looking around in the kitchen, he found some lighter fluid in one of the cabinets under the sink and began squirting it all over the stove and wooden cabinets. After turning the stove on, he ran toward the back door as the flames fed off the wood, quickly spreading the fire throughout the house. Flipping his collar up on his jacket, Trust faded back into the night as the flames burned through the roof of the house, lighting up the night.

Amy pulled up to the police impound where they had taken the bus after the fiasco at the bus station. She saw that there was one officer guarding the lot. It was a young female cop. *If it were a man, I probably could have used my charm,* Amy thought, getting out of the car and heading toward the booth. In the distance, she could see the bus, crashed up, sitting in the corner of the lot away from the other cars.

"Hi, how are you today? I know it's kind of late, but I was wondering if it would be possible for me to grab a few things out of my car that was towed earlier today," Amy said, hoping the officer would go for it.

"We can't let anybody in the lot after hours, ma'am. You can come back tomorrow with the proper paperwork and someone will help you."

"Nobody is even going to know I was back there. I'll only be five minutes if that."

"I'm sorry, ma'am. There's nothing I can do for you. Try back tomorrow," the officer told Amy for the second time.

Amy didn't know what else to say to this woman, and before she turned this into a physical altercation with gunplay, Amy used the one thing any woman couldn't turn down. She reached into her pocketbook and grabbed a stack of money, all hundred-dollar bills. One of two things was going to happen now: either the cop would take the money and let Amy in the lot, or the cop was going to step out of the booth in an attempt to arrest Amy for trying to bribe her.

"This is five thousand dollars," Amy said, slamming the money onto the booth's counter. "All I need is five minutes. After that, you will never see me again. I promise you that," she said, looking the cop in her eyes.

When the cop got out of her seat, Amy reached back into her bag, grabbing her gun, thinking that the cop was going to push her to the limit. It was a relief to Amy when the cop grabbed the money off the counter before coming out of the booth.

"Five minutes," the cop said, leading Amy to the side entrance of the yard.

When Amy got into the yard, she looked back to make sure that the cop wasn't following her, and after seeing that she wasn't being followed, Amy went straight to the bus, looking for a way to get inside without drawing any attention to herself. With the doors smashed in, the only way onto the bus was through the front window, which was missing. She went directly to the right-side rows, tenth seat toward the back, under the cushion of the chair by the window, as Gutta instructed. The diamonds weren't there.

"Lying bastard," Amy mumbled to herself, talking about Gutta.

For the hell of it, she went to the other side of the bus to the same seat closest to the window. "Bingo," Amy mumbled, pulling the small pouch from under the cushion. Dumping some of the diamonds into her hand, Amy just sat there for a few seconds, looking at the diamonds, relieved that they were there. Stuffing them into her pocketbook, Amy got off the bus and walked off the lot, thanking the cop on her way out.

Chapter Sixteen

"Boy, you get more visits than anybody," the guard said jokingly, giving Gutta a pass for visitation.

When he got to the visiting room, he saw Bell sitting in one of the legal booths instead of the special visiting room. She was wearing a tan spaghetti-strap vintage-wash Heartloom Piers dress, a tan jean jacket, and a pair of gold and stacked wood heels with laser-cut detail by Steve Madden. Her hair was pulled back in a ponytail, and she was toting a tan Armani leather-strap bag with cuff bracelets to match.

"I guess I'll be talking to Agent Bell today," Gutta said, coming into the room.

"Naw, nothing has changed. I just thought I'd be a little more professional today being that eyes are everywhere. Did you get a chance to think about what I said to you the other day, or am I still wasting my time?"

"I thought about you. Excuse me. I thought about what you proposed to me," Gutta said, changing up his words, not wanting Bell to know it was really her he was thinking about. Bell smiled at the sound of Gutta trying to switch his words. "Did you get a chance to see the news this morning?"

"No, but I know about those federal agents last night. I guess that takes care of one of your problems," Bell said, looking out at other visitors playing with their children.

Gutta walked up closer to Bell. "I need you to do something for me so I'll know you're not pulling my chain. If you do this, I'll give you the diamonds as long as you get my five million in a week."

"What is it you want me to do?"

"I want you to kill the witness y'all got against me in the triple homicide."

Bell couldn't believe what she'd just heard Gutta say. He wanted her to do something she'd never done before, and that was kill. Not to mention the person he wanted her to kill was only 17. All the money in the world wouldn't bring her to do such a thing. It was bad enough she was beginning to like Gutta on a more personal level.

"I thought you were smarter than that, Gutta. I'm not going that far. You're cute and all, but you're not worth that much. I'll come back some other time when you come up with a better plan than that," she said, grabbing her bag and preparing to stand up.

"Wait! Look, I'll make it easier for you. Just tell me where she's at, and I'll take care of the rest. You don't have to do anything. Hey, you're not giving me much to work with. As long as she can point me out in court, I'll never be free. You and I both know that. I promise this will all be over soon whether you help me or not. I just thought you might want to be on my side of the fence where it's soon to be sunny and sandy," Gutta said, peering into her eyes. Her facial expression softened, and he knew he was wearing her down. "So, are you with me or not? Are you going to let a teenager who couldn't care less about you ruin your chances of becoming a very rich woman?"

His words were slick and convincing to Bell's ears, and for a moment, she forgot she was an agent. This wasn't supposed to be part of her plan, and being this heavily involved made her become just as bad as the people she put in jail. Gutta was working on her, and it was becoming harder to resist the temptation of being a millionaire.

Even more so, it was becoming harder to resist the temptation of him.

"If I tell you where she's at, how can I trust that you won't leave with the diamonds without me?" Bell said, gazing out of the window again.

Gutta walked up close to Bell and grabbed her hand. He raised it to his face and kissed it twice softly before rubbing it on his chest and down his washboard abs. She could feel the ripples through his shirt, and then he planted her hand on his rock-hard dick, allowing her to grab a handful.

"I didn't start off feeling you the way I do now, so you just have to take my word when I tell you we're in this together, and I promise not to dishonor our agreement. Plus, I'm a sucka for sexy-ass FBI agents," Gutta said, smiling at the look on Bell's face as she appeared to be in awe of how big his dick was or his words. He wasn't sure which.

Bell stepped back away from Gutta to avoid any unwanted eyes looking at her. It didn't take long to make her decision, because she began to write down the information he asked for as soon as her hand departed from his dick. Now all Gutta had to do was find someone who would be willing to make the girl disappear off the face of the earth, and with $10 million left at his disposal, it wouldn't be hard.

Agent Ralley pulled up to Monica's house just in time to see them bring her body out along with the body of her husband. They were burnt up pretty bad. The fire trucks finally put the blaze out by the morning, so smoke and fire hoses were everywhere. He was so furious he didn't even bother to ask the officers on the scene what had happened and if there was any evidence found. All he did was stand in the front yard and observe all that was going on. He knew that any chances he had of catching Trust and his crew were gone, and in the process, an agent had been killed, and one was in hot water for being asleep on the job. That meant that Ralley would probably be taken off the case.

His phone began ringing, and he was hesitant to answer it, thinking that it could be bad news. "This is Agent Ralley," he huffed into the phone.

"Agent Ralley, this is Steve, the manager from First Bank. I'm calling about the diamonds. Did you find them yet?"

"No, I haven't, but I assure you that I will do everything in my power to get those diamonds back to you," Ralley said as he watched the coroner bring out the burnt body of the agent. "Just give me a couple more days to check up on these leads I just got," he said, lying, not wanting him to know that his only lead was dead.

As soon as he hung up with the bank manager, he called down to the office and demanded that one of the agents give him all the information on Robert Green they could find. He wanted to know who was investigating his case and who'd been coming to visit him. He wanted to know who he'd been calling, and most important, he wanted him transferred down to the federal detention center by tomorrow. Gutta was his last hope, and he didn't want him getting hurt before he could get another chance to persuade him to cooperate. He told the agent he was talking to to have all that information for him in one hour, knowing that time wasn't on his side.

Chapter Seventeen

A deep sigh left Angela's mouth as she got into her car. She was getting in way too deep with Gutta. Just the thought of him made the hairs on the back of her neck stand up, and she didn't know if it was a good thing or a bad thing. Her senses were reacting either to the danger of him or the attraction she had to him. He was a bad boy to the fullest, the kind who didn't deserve her time, admiration, or attention, but the sight of him made her pussy wet. Angela licked her lips as she pictured her and Gutta somewhere tropical ducked off in a villa, him standing before her naked and ready to devour her body. Her stomach caved in, and she shivered as her phone rang.

Angela threw her head back and looked up at the top of the car. She couldn't even fantasize in peace. After grabbing her phone, she saw that her sister Barbie was calling. "Hey," she answered as she started the car.

"Why have you been so impossible to reach?"

"I've been extremely busy. Do you watch the news?" Angela wasn't being completely truthful with her sister. She had an internal battle going on with herself. A part of her was ashamed of the thoughts she was having of helping Gutta and helping him spend the diamonds that he'd illegally obtained. She'd be throwing away her entire career with one act.

She was so emotional over the entire ordeal that she'd shut herself off from everyone. Angela didn't want to disappoint her parents, and she didn't want to disappoint herself, but those diamonds were calling her. And so was Gutta's dick. She wasn't exactly sure what had come over her, but one thing was for sure: if she didn't soon get a hold of herself, she'd be going down a road she wouldn't be able to come back from.

"Yes, I do," Barbie stated, and her tone held a weird hint of excitement. "One of the alleged bank robbers is the boyfriend of my friend. I just can't believe it. I knew there was something fishy about him. He buys her way too much expensive shit for him to own a convenience store and a few rental properties. One thing I have never been is dumb. Humph."

Angela's brows furrowed. "Have you talked to this friend? Which guy is it?"

"Nope. Faith refuses to answer the phone for me. I'm sure she must be devastated. To know that fine-ass man could be going away for a very long time. Sad."

Barbie didn't sound sad at all. It didn't sound like she knew anything, so there was no need for Angela to try to pry information out of her. Hearing how elated her sister sounded talking about someone else's drama and indiscretions, she knew she had to move very carefully. If she attempted to help Gutta and shit went wrong, she'd for sure be the talk of the town.

Steve, the bank manager, sat in his office after getting off the phone with Agent Ralley and debated whether he should call the owners of the diamonds to let them know that they had been stolen. It was a complicated situation, knowing the capabilities the Russian Kilvalshike family had and how they would react to $20 million in diamonds of theirs coming up missing from his bank.

He finally picked up the phone and dialed the long-distance number to Russia. After a few rings, the phone was picked up by a woman with a Russian accent that Steve was familiar with. It was Jarara, the mistress of the house and also the woman who had flown the diamonds to the United States. Just the sound of her Russian voice sent chills down his spine.

"Hello, this is Steve from the First Bank in the United States. Is Mr. Kilvalshike home?" he asked, stuttering over his words.

There was a moment of silence before Fashkon Kilvalshike, the head of the Russian Mafia, answered the phone. "I was waiting for you to call Steve. I see the news in America from my television set, and your bank is all over it," he said, speaking good English but still with his Russian accent. "I hope you're calling me to tell me that my diamonds are safe."

"Well, you see, sir, that's why I'm calling you. Your diamonds have been stolen in the recent robbery, but the federal government here in the States assured me that they would find them." Steve continued talking until he realized nobody was on the other end of the phone. Kilvalshike had hung up after the word "stolen."

"I thought you told me my diamonds would be safe in America," Fashkon said, sitting back in his love seat with a cigar in his mouth, talking to Jarara. "Come sit next to me," he said in his slow and creepy voice. Doing what she was told, Jarara sat on the floor next to him with her head down, ashamed and afraid to say anything. "Stick out your tongue," he told her while taking a few tokes of his cigar. "I want you to take your sister and go to the States and find my diamonds. You do whatever it takes," he said, putting out the red-hot cigar on her tongue and then shoving it down her throat.

Everybody in Russia knew the Kilvalshike family and how cruel Fashkon could be. He wasn't the type who would just kill you so fast you barely felt any pain, but rather the type who would torture you until you were just about to die. Then he would give you medical attention until you fully recovered and then torture you all over again. He did this to a man about a year ago, and to this day, the man was in Fashkon's basement being tortured every two months.

You would think a little old man of 81 like him would soon die, but not Fashkon. He jogged five miles a day for cardio, did push-ups, pull-ups, and dips for strength, and hunted wild buffalo in the middle of winter for sport. He had only been to the United States one time, and that was to get a Philadelphia cheesesteak he'd heard so much about from a couple of his associates who'd had business there. His empire was Russia, and his diamonds were his pride and joy, kept in the United States for the past year because the Russian government wanted them for themselves due to the history behind them. The government threatened to banish the Kilvalshike family if they were ever found in possession of any of the diamonds.

After the killing at Monica's house, Trust hid out at Amy's house in the Northeast section of Philadelphia. It was there that he got the chance of seeing the diamonds for the first time. Looking at them, he could see how they could be so enticing to have for one's self. He laid them out on the bed, checking the clarity of each one of them one by one.

Amy walked into the room fully dressed. She was on her way to the club to get ready for the night shift. "My cousin called me earlier while you were asleep. She works in the receiving room down at county, and she told me that the Feds were coming to pick up Gutta tomorrow morning and take him to the federal detention center," Amy told Trust.

"I had a feeling they were going to do that. He's all they got. Go ahead and go to work. I'll come by later on tonight to holla at you. I gotta try to catch up with Boom and his boys to see if they want to make some money. Then I got to see if I can find a buyer for these diamonds," Trust said, getting out of the bed in nothing but his boxers, giving Amy an eyeful of his six-pack abs and the bulge from his dick busting out of his boxers.

Boom was Trust's best friend when they were younger, all the way up until Trust stole Amy from him while they were in their late teenage years. It didn't break the friendship between them, but it left a bad taste in Boom's mouth for a couple of years. No matter what the situation was, whenever Trust needed Boom for anything, he was there for him and vice versa. Boom just wasn't down for robbing banks for a living like Trust was. He was more of a street runner. Selling drugs and dog fighting was how he lived, and the whole of Southwest Philly knew and respected him.

"What?" Trust smirked at Amy as she stared at him. She didn't have to respond for him to know what it was. Her eyes said it all, and they held pure lust.

Trust found himself in a hell of a predicament. Amy was his ride or die. No matter how much she still loved him, she put her personal feelings aside and was there any time he needed her. She knew about Faith, and she never gave him grief about it. Instead, she stayed down for him playing her part very well. Trust knew to take it there with her may be asking for trouble, but he was conflicted. It may have sounded cocky, but he damn near reasoned that she should be awarded some kind of affection for her loyalty. She would never completely have his heart, so why not hit her off with some good dick? Shit, if he didn't make it out of the mess he'd gotten into, he wouldn't be getting pussy from Faith, Amy, or anyone else for a long-ass time.

He took a step toward her, and Amy's heart rate increased. Her breath caught in her throat. Was this going to be the moment she'd been yearning for?

Trust's phone rang, and Amy wanted to scream. His gaze shifted toward the screen, and when he went to answer it, her heart dropped. The moment was ruined. So he wouldn't see the disappointment in her eyes, she simply turned and left the room so she could go to work.

"Hey, babe," Trust answered Faith while watching Amy walk away. "Yo, where are you?" he asked, happy to hear her voice.

"We're in Georgia right now. We should be in Florida by tomorrow morning," Faith answered, but she was not in a good mood.

"What's wrong? You sound upset about something."

"It's Zoe. He left the hotel sometime during the night, and we can't find him anywhere. He turned off his cell phone so we couldn't call him. All night while I was driving, he talked about you and how much he loves you. I think he might be on his way back to the city."

"Damn, Zoe," Trust mumbled to himself. "All right, I'll keep an eye out for him in case he comes back. You just make it to Florida and call me when you get there."

"What am I supposed to do when I get to Florida? I don't know anybody down there."

"Start looking for a house, something in the two hundred K area," Trust said before hanging up the phone. Once they ended the call, Trust called Boom.

The phone rang a couple of times before Boom finally answered. "Hell must have frozen over if you took the time to pick up the phone and call ya boy," Boom answered jokingly, because he hadn't heard from Trust in a couple of months.

"Don't do me like that, playboy. What's good with ya?" Trust shot back.

"You know, same shit different toilet. What you got for me? 'Cause I know you're calling me for something, and if you're calling me, I know it's about some paper."

"Yeah, well, I'm not going to do too much talking over the jack. You still on Fifty-eighth Street?"

"What you talking about? Dis my hood. I'm not going nowhere no matter how much money I get," Boom said, taking another puff of the Dutch he was smoking.

"I'll be through there in about an hour. I'm not in my car, so tell ya young bucks I'm coming. I don't want to have to leave ya block filled with teddy bears and candles," Trust joked, but in a sense, he was serious knowing how ruthless Boom's crew was.

It'd been a while since Trust had been in the hood. He really didn't have to go, considering his line of work and the amount of money he was getting from it. But he always tried to keep his ear to the streets, just to stay up on what was new, who had died, who'd had a baby, and who had gone to jail. Even though he'd left the hood, the hood remained in him, something that could never be taken away from him by a couple of nice cars, a condo in the suburbs, a nurse for a girlfriend, and a cat named Mr. Bogus. You could always take the nigga out of the hood, but you could never take the hood out of the nigga.

After all the mayhem Trust was causing in the streets of Philly, it was time to leave the hood for good this time. With the cops patrolling the streets all day and night and his face all over the news, being armed and dangerous, the Feds searching high and low, suspecting him as the culprit for the massacre at Monica's house, it wouldn't be long until Faith would be identifying his body in the morgue or visiting him in prison. Little did the city know, Trust was just getting started turning the city upside down.

Chapter Eighteen

Trust was cautious driving through the city on his way to see Boom. When he pulled up to the block, everything and everybody was moving so fast it scared Trust. Crackheads were lined up against the wall, the Chinese store on the corner was packed with people, young girls were walking down the street with hardly anything on, and lookouts were posted in different areas, including on the roofs, all of whom were armed with choppers. In the middle of all the activity stood Boom, a skinny black nigga with braids, surrounded by a bunch of goons. With the naked eye you wouldn't see Boom as a threat. In fact, one probably wouldn't see Boom at all. He packed a mean bite with no bark. He stood at the top of the steps, wearing a black dickey and a pair of tan Timberland boots.

When Trust walked up the street after parking his car two blocks away, a couple of guys standing on the steps with Boom pulled out their guns at the unfamiliar face approaching. Boom quickly checked his boys, telling them to stand down. Trust smiled at the sight of his good friend. In a way he was proud of how far Boom had come, from the times when they used to share and wear each other's clothes, to school, to becoming a boss.

"Damn, boy, you know a nigga got to be on point with a black nigga like you walking down the street," Boom joked. "You look like you about to kill somebody," he said, getting off the steps and giving Trust a hug.

"I been puttin' work in all week," Trust said while being led into the house.

"Yeah, I know. I been watching the news. I saw 'em running up in that house you had on the ave."

Trust looked shocked that Boom knew the house on Chester Avenue was his.

"Shit, I know everything that goes on in my hood," he told Trust, who was looking surprised. "I told you about that bank robbery shit, my nig. That shit is only good for a couple of times. After that you gotta get out," Boom went on, giving his friend an earful. "Now tell me what I can do for you."

Trust reached in his pocket and pulled out the only diamond he'd brought with him, and he tossed it to Boom. "You tryin' to make some money?" Trust asked Boom, who was stuck looking at the size of the diamond.

"What kind of money?" Boom asked, not being able to take his eyes off the diamond.

"I need some major work put in, plus a buyer for a couple million dollars' worth of diamonds. If you willing to ride out with me, I got two million for you either in diamonds or in cash, whichever one you want," Trust said, giving Boom eye-to-eye contact to let him know the seriousness of the situation.

"I told you, Trust, I don't do banks. I sell drugs."

"It doesn't have anything to do with banks. I promise you. "

"Fuck it. Fill me in on what you got," Boom said, giving Trust his undivided attention.

Amy had been trying to call Trust all night, but he wasn't answering the phone at all. Agent Ralley had been snooping around the club for the past hour, and not once did he look at or talk to any of the strippers. When he first walked into the club, he began asking Amy about her relationship with Robert "Gutta" Green and why she had gone to visit him. The office had called Ralley and given him all the information about who was going to visit Gutta and who he was calling. Amy told him that Gutta was an old boyfriend, and she just went to see how he was doing. But that wasn't enough, because he hadn't left the club yet.

Earlier that day, Ralley met up with Agent Bell to find out her status on the case concerning Gutta. She gave him bits and pieces just to get him out of her office. She could tell by the way he was asking questions that he was up to something, but she couldn't figure out what it was. His questions were limited while standing in front of Special Agent Coles, the head of the FBI and the one every agent had to answer to. Coles was probably the only agent in the bureau who wasn't crooked, and the last person you would want to be investigating you.

It wasn't long before Trust came walking through the doors of the club just like he said he would. Amy tried to say something to him before he could reach the bar, but he sat right next to Agent Ralley, who was drinking a glass of water.

"Sorry, sir, you can't buy the dancers a drink," Amy said to Trust, cutting her eyes at Agent Ralley in hopes that he would catch on. "Sir, you can't sit there," she informed Trust, seeing that he didn't catch the first warning.

By then it was too late. Ralley caught on before Trust did. He looked over and saw that it was him. To be sure, Ralley took a double take, and then looked to his inside jacket pocket where he kept a picture of Trust, Gutta, and Zoe. To his surprise, he was sitting right next to the infamous Darien "Trust" Walker, which was his birth name. After slowly putting down the cup of water and preparing for the confrontation, Ralley reached for his gun, turned around, and pointed it at Trust's face.

"FBI! You better not think about moving!" Ralley yelled out, now getting Trust's attention.

It was only the sound of Amy cocking a shotgun that caught the attention of some of the customers along with Ralley, as she pointed it directly to the side of Ralley's head. The club that was once so loud became so quiet you could hear an ant piss on cotton. The DJ had turned the music off and got everybody's attention. People who were sitting on the stools at the bar slowly got up and got lost. Trust just sat at the bar without even picking his head up to look at the agent but noticing the long pump shotgun pointing directly at the man. Agent Ralley had become more afraid for his own life but wasn't willing to back down.

"I guess we got ourselves a situation," Trust said, turning around on his stool to face Ralley. "The way I see it is you got two options," Trust began. "One, you can pull the trigger, killing me, then get your own head blown off. Or two, you can put ya gun back in ya holster and walk out of here alive and try to catch me on another date, which I highly doubt," Trust said, reaching to grab his drink from the bar, downing the double shot of vodka in front of him.

Agent Ralley thought about it, turning his head to look down the barrel of Amy's shotgun, seeing that she was firm and fixed on her position. Lowering his weapon, Ralley complied with option number two.

"You know you're not going to get away. No matter where you go, I'll be on your tail. And now that you have seen me and I have seen you, it evens out the playing field," Ralley said, getting off his stool and walking toward the exit.

It was burning Ralley up, letting the most wanted man in the city of Philadelphia go and still not being able to get the diamonds. He knew that Trust had killed Monica, her husband, and the federal agent, and it was too much to just let it go. Ralley got to the section where the booths were and drew his weapon, spinning around and firing several shots in the direction of Trust and Amy. The bullets broke bottles behind the bar and shattered mirrors along the walls. The people who were still in the club began running out the front door, knocking each other over trying to duck the flying bullets passing over their heads. An off-duty cop who was armed with his gun joined sides with Ralley and took cover behind one of the booths.

Amy was the first to fire back, blasting chips of wood from the booth onto the heads of Ralley and the cop. Back-to-back, shots spit out of Amy's chrome pump, just missing her target. Trust ran to the other side of the room to get a better shot, releasing four quick rounds from his double-action .50-caliber Desert Eagle that had an extended clip. Ralley ran for cover after barely dodging the bullets breezing by his head.

Jumping up from behind the booth, the off-duty cop was met by Trust, who was walking down the top of the connecting booths with rapid fire, hitting the cop in the stomach and the chest. Firing at Amy running behind the bar for cover, Ralley quickly turned his attention to Trust, knocking him off the booth with a single shot to the chest. The fatal shot only turned out to be a bruise because Trust had on the vest that Amy had given him the other day. Reloading his gun and cocking it before pointing it at Trust, Ralley could see a shadow in his peripheral view. When he turned to see who it was, the blast from the shotgun lifted him off his feet from a close-range shot to the chest. The blast knocked him into the air and onto a table, and he broke it on his way to the ground.

"Get up," Amy said, helping Trust to his feet and leading him to the back door.

Looking at her small club for the last time, Amy closed the back door behind her, knowing that she could never step foot back inside of it. Now, just like the rest of the crew, she was on the run from the law.

Angela sat at home all night thinking about Gutta and all the possibilities for them if they could actually get away. Over the past few months, she'd studied his life and the way he lived it, strictly about his business and not up for too many games. He was a gangsta, and although she was a Fed, those were the kind of men Angela had always been attracted to. She was born in West Philly, also known as "the bottom," but moved to North Philly when she was about 2 years old. Her parents were struggling when they first got married, but after leaving college and beginning promising careers, it didn't take long for their tax bracket to change. Angela grew up very privileged. After a few failed relationships, she actually thought that throwing herself into her work would be fulfilling. But after being alone for the past few years, not committing herself to any relationships, she found it harder living without a companion she could come home to at night. The Fed life was not all she thought it would be, but rather it became very time consuming.

As she lay in bed watching the news, the top story of the day came over the TV screen. It quickly caught her attention, getting her to sit up in bed and turn up the volume.

"A shoot-out at a Main Street lounge left an off-duty cop dead and an FBI agent hospitalized. The story is still developing as to what took place. Officer Trenton Hicks was pronounced dead at the scene from several fatal shots. Most of the witnesses left the club before the gun battle began, and those who were there are being questioned by the authorities. The name of the FBI agent has not been released. We'll keep you informed as the story unfolds," the news anchor announced before going to commercial.

Angela wasted no time turning off the TV and picking up the phone to find out the name of the hospitalized agent.

Chapter Nineteen

Trust and Amy used fake IDs to check into a hotel, the Moon, in West Philadelphia, somewhere nobody would suspect them to be. The staff there didn't look at the news frequently enough to know what was going on or who they were. The hotel was pretty old and dirty, with crackheads and prostitutes lingering around the premises. It wasn't the ideal place they wanted to be, but for the moment, it was the perfect spot to hide out.

They got into the room, immediately stripped the bed of its linens, and replaced them with the brand-new ones Trust grabbed from the closet in the hallway on his way upstairs, along with a bottle of disinfectant. For about an hour, they both cleaned the hell out of that room, especially the bathroom, because a shower was badly needed after all that had happened today. They didn't plan to stay there long, but while they were there, they were going to make sure it was clean.

Trust took off his vest and could see the bruise caused by Ralley shooting him. He iced it while Amy was taking a shower. He was really feeling the way Amy had his back in the club, thinking that if it weren't for her, he would probably be dead or in jail right now.

"Thank you," Trust told Amy as she was coming out of the bathroom with only a towel wrapped around her body.

"Thanks for what?"

"You know, for holding me down back there."

All Amy could do was smile. "You just don't get it, do you? I'm always going to hold you down," she said, sitting down on the bed next to him. "Do you remember when we were together and my family didn't want us to be together?"

"Yeah, I remember."

"Do you remember what I told you the night that you broke up with me?"

"You told me that no matter how long it took, you were gonna wait for me. You said that you'd always be there for me no matter what."

"Nothing has changed, Trust. I will always have your back, and I will always love you through hell and back," she said, leaning in to kiss him on the cheek.

Just that small kiss brought back so many memories in Trust's mind that he leaned over to kiss her back, but he stopped when the thought of Faith flashed in his head. He wanted so badly to make love to Amy, and by the hardness of his dick, he surely wasn't the only one.

"I got to get in the shower," Trust said, ruining the mood and putting out the flames of what was once true fire between him and Amy.

Trust jumped in the shower, using all cold water in hopes that it would cool him down. He couldn't help but think about how good Amy looked with just a towel wrapped around her body and her hair slightly wet from the shower. As he sat there and thought about her, Amy came into the bathroom and pulled the shower curtain to the side, getting Trust's attention.

She slowly undid her towel. It dropped to the floor, leaving her standing there in front of him, completely naked. Trust couldn't help but stand to the side and let her climb in. He couldn't fight it if he tried. She grabbed a hold of his wrist and pulled him closer to her. Her body was the same as Trust left it two years ago: flawless. Her

breasts showed no signs of sagging, her stomach was flat
and toned, her pussy was shaved bald, her thighs were
thick as ever, her ass was fat and juicy, and the touch
of her skin was ever so soft. She was a sad reminder of
a good thing. Without a word being said, he could hold
back no further, gazing into her eyes and kissing her soft,
full lips. It was everything he was missing and all that he
wanted at the moment.

He turned off the shower, grabbing her hand and
leading her to the bed with lustful eyes. He didn't have
to not think about Faith. Looking at Amy made him
forget all about her, at least for now. Slowly he laid her
onto the bed, climbing on top of her and giving her small
kisses to her lips and neck, fondling her breast in the
process. Doing so made her pussy wet. When he took in
a mouthful of her breast, she moaned at the warmness
of his tongue licking around her nipple, leaving the cool
sensation of wetness on one titty as he moved on to the
other one.

"I missed you," she said softly, grabbing Trust's head
and guiding it on her breast.

His warm kisses didn't stop there as he led a trail
of them down the center of her stomach, reaching her
thighs, biting both of them lightly before stuffing his
tongue inside of her wet box. It damn near made Amy
cum instantly. She tasted so good, and all Amy could do
was grab a handful of the back of Trust's head, enjoying
the super sensation of Trust's tongue swiping across
her pussy lips and around her clit. She almost ripped
the sheets off the bed, trying her best to get away from
Trust's mouth. The things Trust did with his tongue gave
Amy multiple orgasms. This was the desire both of them
had felt and wanted, and finally they were making it a
reality after all this time.

He finally lifted his head up from Amy's wet box, wiping the lather of her cum off his face with the washrag he'd brought from the bathroom. Now climbing on top of her in missionary, the tip of his rock-hard dick pierced her womb, causing her to pant out how good he felt inside of her. With only a quarter of his dick inside of her, she held on tight, wrapping her arms around his back and trying to hold on for dear life. When he shoved the last four inches of his dick inside of her, she bit the side of his neck and sucked on it at the same time, moaning loudly and uncontrollably. His strokes were slow and deep, and the farther he went inside of her, the wetter she got. His manhood was penetrating things inside of Amy that hadn't been touched in ages, and from the way things felt, Trust knew that she wasn't lying when she said she wasn't having sex with anybody.

Throughout the night, Trust made love to Amy just the way she wanted it, thus fulfilling any sexual desire she had that had grown over the years. Trust was also pleased, cummin' inside of her, sharing the fluids of pleasure repeatedly while the night went on.

Jamita and Jarara landed in Philadelphia around 7:00 p.m., turning heads as they walked through the airport like a pair of runway models. White but tanned well, Jamita stood six feet tall. She was thin and had long blond hair that came down to her butt. She was wearing all black: patent leather thigh-high boots and a black miniskirt with matching top. Her eyes were covered with a pair of light pink Gucci glasses, and she carried a Gucci leather-strap tote bag. Chewing a piece of bubble gum, she managed to avoid smearing her lip gloss, which made her lips look juicy. Her hips slammed side to side like she was missing a bone, and being that she wasn't carrying any luggage, everyone got the full effect of her stride.

Jarara also turned heads, wearing a pair of nude Louboutin heels, a pair of tight, fitted denim jeans, and a belly shirt that showed off her flat stomach. Her hair was in a ponytail draped down the center of her back, and her petite five-foot-five-inch body was well proportioned on every level. She kinda had a body like a Southern black girl, thick to death.

It was like slow motion watching them come through the airport, and their swagger made some people think that they were famous or at least someone important. Not famous in America, but well known in Russia, the two of them were far from innocent or sweet. They were two of Russia's quietest assassins, happy and pleased to do anything for Fashkon. They were in the States for one reason and one reason only, and that was to get Fashkon's diamonds back or die trying, killing anybody who stood in their way, including the authorities.

Chapter Twenty

"Green, pack ya shit. You're outta here today!" the guard yelled into the pod.

"Out of here? Where the hell am I going?" Gutta said, looking confused as to why and where he was going.

Once in the receiving room, Gutta was met by two well-dressed men in suits flashing their FBI badges. Gutta immediately thought about Bell and wondered if she knew they were coming today. The whole time in the receiving room, neither one of the agents said a word to Gutta, nor did they answer the many questions he was asking.

Gutta was escorted out of county and placed into an unmarked federal Crown Vic with black tinted windows. On the expressway, the two agents sped in the passing lane at eighty miles per hour. Gutta noticed the escorts, two black SUVs, with them: one behind them and the other one speeding up in front of them. The traffic was kind of congested coming off the expressway by Eighth Street, and when the Feds got off and turned down Eighth Street, they pulled right in front of one of the SUVs Gutta noticed from the expressway. The other SUV pulled right up behind them. At the corner of the block there was a bus stop, which was about fifteen feet from the light that just turned red.

Between the cars on the other side of the two-way lane, the SUV in front of them, and the SUV behind them, the agents were totally surrounded and pretty much pinned in. Without warning, the two back doors from the SUV in front of them swung open, and out jumped two masked gunmen armed with AR-15 assault rifles. Seeing this, the agent quickly tried to put his car in reverse, only to crash into the SUV behind them. The two men jumped on top of the hood of the Crown Vic, pointing their guns at the agents, military style, making the agents think twice about pulling their weapons.

"Get ya hands where I can see them!" one of the gunmen yelled out.

The driver from the first SUV also got out of the car, only to hold the first car in the second lane at gunpoint so no traffic would be able to move when the light turned green.

Standing at the bus stop, Trust walked over to the passenger side of the federal car and broke the window out, punching through it with his gun clutched in his hand. Boom, the driver of the second SUV, behind the car, joined Trust in disarming the federal agents, taking the keys out of the ignition at the same time so the car wouldn't be able to move. The men worked and moved so fast that half of the drivers packed on Eighth Street didn't even know what was going on. The drivers who did see what was going on were in awe at the sight of the large guns the men possessed.

Opening the back door to the federal car, Trust grabbed Gutta and escorted him quickly to the second SUV, tossing him into the back seat. The agents stood stiff as the men, one by one, got back into the SUVs, but not before taking the keys from the driver of the first car in the second lane so no traffic would be able to move at all on Eighth Street. Boom, in the second SUV, drove up onto the sidewalk to get around the federal car, which couldn't

move. Not one shot had to be fired, and that was planned
for a reason. Sitting across the street about one block
over was Roundhouse Police Station, the main station in
Philadelphia.

While sitting in the back seat, Gutta didn't say a word
as Trust began taking off the leg irons, freeing Gutta from
the custody of the law. Like always, the getaway was the
most important part of the job, and who was better in
charge than Trust to come up with that plan? First, the
two SUVs split up in two different directions, but both
had the same plan. After getting a nice distance away
from the federal agents, one person at a time would get
out of the truck on a corner where the El train was running, giving them access to the public transportation
without drawing a lot of attention to them. Gutta, of
course, couldn't be left alone, and frankly he didn't want
to be considering that he along with Trust were the most
wanted men in the city of Philadelphia, if not the
most wanted men in America.

The sound of cop cars rang out throughout downtown
in search of two black SUVs. The cops pulled over every
SUV they came in contact with, and by the time they
finally caught up with the ones that were used in the
escape, they were abandoned with little to no evidence of
who was in them.

The job was successful. Trust had done it again. With
the help of an old friend and a couple of his boys, he
managed to make the city even hotter now, leaving a
blemish on the federal system's inmate-transportation
policy. With someone as dangerous as Gutta coming to
the Feds, they were supposed to have more manpower
guarding him during the transfer. Just like that, in less
than sixty seconds, the streets got one up on the Feds,
showing them that they weren't the only ones with power.

***

Agent Ralley was in the hospital cursing up a storm when he got the word that Gutta was taken from the Feds. If it weren't for the shootout the night before, it would have been him going to get Gutta from county. The only thing that saved his life was the large bulletproof vest he had on that had caught the buckshot from Amy's gun but left him with a few broken ribs and a headache. This had become so personal to Ralley. He no longer wanted to see the whole crew in jail but rather floating in the Delaware River. Getting the diamonds was a must at this point as well, seeing as though the bureau was sure to retire him now after the incident last night.

Ralley got up to get dressed in an attempt to leave the hospital when he was interrupted by two men with high-priced suits coming into the room flashing Internal Affairs badges.

"Agent Ralley, I'm Inspector Holloway and this is Inspector Goodell. We want to talk to you about what happened last night if you don't mind."

"Yeah, well, I really couldn't tell you what happened. The blast kind of knocked my screws loose," Ralley said, putting on his shirt, not willing to share any information.

Seeing how he reacted, Holloway got more specific with his questioning. "I'm sure you're familiar with Robert 'Gutta' Green, Darien 'Trust' Walker, and Rodney 'Zoe' Swinton," Holloway said, throwing their photos on the bed. "And I guess you also know about the snatch and grab job this morning with Gutta."

"Look, I've been chasing these guys around for months, trying to use every clue from every robbery to find them, and up until a couple of weeks ago, they were ghosts."

Ralley started telling them about the robbery and the death of his witness and how Gutta was his last hope. He told them things he thought they wanted to hear but left out a lot of things he thought they shouldn't know about, like the diamonds.

"Look, Agent Ralley, you guys better get some control over what's going on in this city, or I'll see to it that the FBI will all be investigated before the year is out. And if I find out you're not telling me something, and another law enforcement officer so much as gets a scratch on him over these three men you're chasing around, I will personally hold you responsible," Holloway said before storming out of the room.

When the news of Gutta's escape got to Angela, all she could do was smile out of both anger and happiness. For starters, she was upset that he didn't trust her enough to tell her about the escape, but on the other hand, she was happy he got away. The phone in her office had been ringing off the hook with other agents wanting to know what had happened. She even got a visit from IA, Holloway and Goodell, who did a lot of snooping around in her personal life. That was all IA was good for, investigating crooked cops and Feds.

So much had gone on in the federal building in the past hour, Bell just decided to take the rest of the day off to avoid all the questions she had coming at her. She didn't even take time out to interview the two agents who were transporting Gutta. Now it was up to Gutta to make contact with her, and when he did, she would be ready for him, having found a Cuban buyer for the diamonds.

Changing motels early this morning, Amy found herself feeling energetic for some odd reason. Who was she kidding? She knew there was one man who could make her feel this way, and that was Trust. It felt so good

but then so bad when she came back to reality and remembered that he belonged to someone else. In fact,
according to him, he was about to marry her.

*He didn't say a word when he got up and left this
morning,* she thought, lying in bed, changing the chan-
nels, trying to catch the news. If there was one thing she
knew about Trust, it was that he had a big heart, and the
only time she could tell he felt guilty about something
was when he was silent or his conversation was a mere
few words.

Jamita wasted little time, walking through the doors of
First Bank, immediately grabbing the attention of Steve,
the bank's manager. He rushed out of his office to meet
and greet her, directing her to his office.

"Who has my diamonds?" she asked with a strong
Russian accent, twirling her chewing gum around her
finger, looking around the office.

"The FBI assured me that they would get the diamonds
back. Apparently, some street thugs robbed the bank and
took the diamonds, and they had help from one of our
employees, Monica."

"Where is this Monica person?"

"She was killed along with her husband and a federal
agent a couple of nights ago. She identified the robbers
before she was killed. Agent Ralley was the one in charge
of the whole investigation. He knows exactly who got the
diamonds."

For the next half hour, Steve broke down and told
Jamita everything he knew about the robbery, including every detail of how they came in and how they got
away. He made sure he gave her Ralley's contact information. Standing up to close the blinds on the office door,
Jamita popped bubbles with her gum, reaching for her

gun in her thigh-high boots. Steve was shocked, wanting to call out for help, but he couldn't find the words to say, hoping she wouldn't pull the trigger. His hopes fell short when Jamita fired two shots into his chest that were muffled by a silencer, leaving him laid out in his chair. Jamita then took the DO NOT DISTURB sign he had hanging on the wall and placed it on the doorknob as she left the office. She went out the front doors of the bank, leaving no indication to the rest of the employees doing their normal operations that anything had gone on.

The information she got from Steve would come in handy later as she tracked down the diamonds and eliminated any witnesses she came across. Ralley had become her new target. Based on any information he gave her, she would move on to the next piece of the puzzle until she found who and what she was looking for, unwilling to leave the States alive without Fashkon's diamonds.

Chapter Twenty-one

Trust and Gutta walked into the hotel room where Amy was, surprising her because she had no idea about the plan to get Gutta from the Feds. Acknowledging Amy but wanting to get out of his prison uniform, Gutta went into the bathroom with the change of clothes Trust had waiting for him.

"No, you didn't," Amy whispered, getting off the bed and walking up to Trust, pointing her finger at the bathroom. "Why didn't you tell me you were breaking him out today?" she continued in a whisper while looking at the bathroom door to see if it was closed all the way.

"If I had told you, you would have wanted to come, so I let you stay here, asleep, where it was safe."

"Why?" she asked.

"No matter what Gutta does in his spare time, he's still a part of my crew. You of all people should know that when I give my word, I stick to it. Plus, the money I paid to get him out is coming out of his pocket. I'm sure two million was worth his freedom."

"What about the diamonds?"

"I'm waiting for Boom to call me back. He said he might know someone who would buy some of them. I figure a couple million for now would get us far away from here. I'ma get Gutta out of the city, and then after that he can do whatever he wants with his money."

"What about us?" Amy said, thinking about last night and what was going to happen now.

Trust sat on the bed and began scratching his head in deep thought, not prepared to answer the question. He started to feel torn between the two women, being that he loved each of them for different reasons. Amy was his first love, but Faith was his new love. The only reason he wasn't with Amy was because he thought what he did was the right thing for her and her family when he broke up with her. And for a while, he regretted it, breaking the heart of someone who truly loved him. Faith, on the other hand, was everything he expected to find after Amy. It took him a while to get over Amy and to find it in his heart to love someone else, but he finally did, appreciating and understanding the love Faith had for him.

"I don't know about us right now, Amy. I mean, last night was official, but the fact still remains that I got a fiancée, and I already cheated on her twice," he said, referring to Monica being the first.

Amy started to say something, but Gutta came back into the room with his new clothes on. "So, what now?" he asked Trust, not knowing he'd just butted in on a deep conversation.

"Look, we're all hot as fish grease right now, so the best thing to do is chill out for a couple days 'til the heat cools down in the streets. Cops are going to be everywhere, all day, all night with a copy of our pictures sitting on the dashboard. When it cools down, you can get the rest of the diamonds, I can see about getting a sale for them, and then we can get da fuck out of here for good. Shit!" Trust screamed out. "Zoe left the hotel yesterday. Faith said she thinks he's on his way back to the city," he said, pulling out his phone in an attempt to call him, but Zoe's phone was still turned off. "I got to keep my eyes open for him. I think I might know the first place he's going."

"Yo, Wanda took the money I had at the crib and did a disappearing act with it. All I got is the diamonds."

Trust went in the dresser drawer and grabbed a stack of money but put it back after a quick thought of Gutta trying to leave the city on his own. "Don't worry about money right now, 'cause you don't need it. Amy's gonna get another room so you can stay in, and here's a couple bucks so you can order takeout," Trust said, passing Gutta $50. "I don't want you out on the streets. The next time you go to jail, I promise I'll let you stay."

Amy pointed at the TV as breaking news broadcast over the show she had been watching. None other than Gutta's face covered the screen, warning the city of his escape and how to contact the police if anyone were to see him. They talked about checkpoints set up around the city for identification checks and how the Philadelphia police were teaming with the FBI in a manhunt for Gutta. The news anchor went on to say that there was a connection between Gutta, Trust, and Zoe, who were also possible suspects in the armed bank robbery of First Bank a couple of weeks ago. They were flashing Trust's picture along with Zoe's over the screen. The news just kept pouring in with story after story.

"This woman, twenty-seven-year-old Amanda Young, the owner of Stars Coffee and Lounge, was reported missing after a gun battle erupted at the lounge last night around ten o'clock between an unidentified suspect and police," the news anchor reported. "If you see her, contact the missing persons unit at . . ."

Trust looked at Amy in a confused way, wondering what was going on. He was sure that Agent Ralley would have said something by now about what had happened, but evidently he hadn't, according to the news report. As of now, Amy wasn't wanted. She was just missing. But Trust wasn't taking any chances of that being totally true and exposing Amy to the public. He wasn't sure whether it was a trick to lure her out and arrest her on sight.

"This developing story is also underway. The manager of First Bank was found this afternoon in his office shot to death. Nobody knew how long he had been in there, but the medical examiner reported him dead at the scene," the news anchor went on. "We'll bring you more on this story as it unfolds."

Now everybody in the room looked around at each other, seeing if anybody had an answer for that crazy piece of news. Gutta quickly said that he was with Trust all morning when Amy looked his way with one eyebrow up. Normally all eyes would be looking at Gutta for something like this, and this may have been the only time he had a good alibi for his whereabouts. The manager's death just made things a lot more confusing, especially since the FBI agent hadn't locked Amy up for the shooting. They all sat in the room stumped, scratching their heads as the news anchor continued with the broadcast.

"We have a severe thunderstorm warning for tonight and well throughout the rest of the weekend," she said, turning it over to the weatherman.

Just when Trust thought things couldn't get any worse, his phone began to ring. It was Zoe, and he was back in the city.

It started raining cats and dogs, and Ralley finally made it home after spending hours at the bank investigating Steve's death, wondering why somebody would kill him. Not just kill him, but do it while he was at work. The video footage from the bank showed a white woman leaving his office last. Her sunglasses covered half her face, so facial recognition was ruled out.

Ralley sat at his computer going over the crew's file, hoping to find something that could help him figure out their possible next move before they fled the city with

$20 million in diamonds. He also tapped into the bank's files to find out more information about the diamonds, who they belonged to, and why they were in that bank. It took most of the night researching the information. This was probably the most FBI work he had done in a long time, so much that he nodded off at the computer.

Click! The sound of a large revolver to the back of his head woke him up, startling him as he opened his eyes to see the reflection of a woman in his computer screen.

"Where are my diamonds?" a Russian female voice asked, pressing the .38 Special against the back of his head.

"I don't know where the diamonds are, lady. I don't know who you think you are coming into my home pointing a gun at me, but I am an FBI agent."

That didn't matter to Jamita, who he was or how he felt. Pressing the gun harder against his head, Jamita demanded to know about the information Steve had told her. When he refused, Jamita grabbed him by the back of his collar and dragged him to the floor and handcuffed him with the cuffs that were sitting next to his gun on the side of the computer. With her gun in one hand, she dragged Ralley across the room and tossed him onto the bed so he was facing her. Knowing a thing or two about torture and how the human male body works, she stood back, holstered her gun inside of her boot, and began snatching off his pants, leaving his bottom half-naked. Pulling out a butterfly knife from her other boot, she climbed on top of Ralley, stabbing the knife into the bed beside him. Ralley had no idea what was about to happen to him, thinking the worst.

Jamita leaned over to whisper in his ear. "You're going to tell me what I want to know one way or the other," she said, making her way down to his dick and then taking him into her mouth.

The old man's dick got hard, and his confusion was overcome by the pleasure of Jamita's warm mouth swallowing the whole of his dick, sucking on it at a slow pace. It had been a long time since he'd had his dick sucked, and coming from a pretty young girl was a bonus, for now.

"Robert Green, Darien Walker, and Rodney Swinton," Ralley began to talk. "They're bank robbers, and I think they have the diamonds," he said, barely able to get his words out. "All . . . all the information I've got on them is over there on the computer."

Not all forms of torture had to be painful, as long as what you were doing short-circuited the mind, leaving it vulnerable and unable to process what came out of the mouth. This form of torture was called pleasurable torture, which, with Jamita, always ended in pain. As the sounds of spit swished around his dick, Ralley was on the verge of cummin' when, out of nowhere, Jamita rose, grabbed the knife out of the bed, cut his dick clean off with one swipe, and stuffed it into his mouth. As he screamed, Jamita pulled the .38 from her boot and fired a single shot to his forehead, splattering his brains on the pillow. She stood over his lifeless body, wiping the spit from the corner of her mouth, smiling, and holding a crazy look in her eyes.

Picking the chair up and sitting at the computer, Jamita looked through everything he had on the crew, not at all bothered by the dead man with a dick stuffed in his mouth lying right behind her.

"Gutta, Trust, and Zoe. What kinds of silly American names are these?" Jamita mumbled to herself, staring into the computer. "All of you will die."

Trust left the hotel to meet up with Boom about the guy who wanted to buy just a few of the diamonds. As he sat down in the back of the bus, his phone began to ring. It was Faith. "Hey, babe," Trust answered, happy to hear from her.

"I'm in Florida now. We got here earlier today, but I checked into a hotel and got some sleep. Baby, I miss you. When am I going to see you?"

"Soon. As soon as the time is right, I'ma get out of here. There's just a lot of police everywhere."

"Do you have time to talk?" Faith asked, wanting to know what was going on.

"Yeah, I got some time. What's on ya mind?"

"All of this, Trust. You tell me not to worry, but how can I not? I don't know what you're there doing. I just know that I'm supposed to trust you. I don't nag you because I want your head to be as clear as it can so you can think, but I'm scared."

"Listen, I can't make any promises. You made it to Florida safely, and that's all I care about. I love you, and I love my unborn child. With everything in me, I'm going to fight to get to where you are. Okay?"

"Okay," Faith mumbled. Trust knew she wasn't pleased, but there wasn't anything else he could do about it.

Trust coddled Faith for a few more seconds, and as soon as their call ended, the phone rang again. He thought she may have called him back, but he looked down at the phone, and to his surprise, it was Zoe calling. He knew that no matter what he told Zoe, the man wouldn't be able to stay away.

"Yo," he answered and paused to make sure that it was really Zoe on the other end of the phone.

"What's good, G?"

Trust gave Zoe an address to meet him at later. *No sense in trying to do everything alone.* This was a mess that they could only get out of if they worked together.

Chapter Twenty-two

Picking the phone up on the first ring, seeing that it was indeed Fashkon, Jamita began informing him of what was going on in the States. Not caring anything about what she was saying, Fashkon asked one question, "Do you have my diamonds?" and when she said no, he hung up the phone without saying another word.

That was enough to fuel more flames inside of Jamita. Hearing Fashkon's voice was like putting a battery in her back, and the thought of disappointing him made her go even harder. Returning to Russia without the diamonds wasn't even considered, because if she went back there empty-handed, it could very well cost her her life.

Jamita was deeply indebted to Fashkon. There was no running from him. His power and his reach were long. The only option she had was making him happy. There was nothing else. She had to be thorough, and she had to be strategic. Jamita was literally fighting for her life when it came to dealing with Fashkon. Being on his bad side was nothing short of being in a living hell. The Americans who had taken the diamonds thought they were smart, but she was going to have to be even smarter.

Amy walked over to Gutta's room to see if he wanted something to eat, because she was about to order out. When she got there, he wasn't in the room, and it looked like he'd been gone for a while. She immediately called

Trust, who didn't answer the phone at first. She tried right back again, and he answered.

"Gutta left his room!" Amy yelled into the phone. "I don't know where he went or how long he's been gone!"

"Calm down, calm down. He probably went to get somethin' to eat. Give him some time. If he doesn't come back in about an hour, then call me back. He couldn't have gone far with fifty bucks."

"He might have gone to get those diamonds," she said, leaving his room.

"If Gutta wants to go to jail, then that's on him. You just make sure you stay put. I'll call you back," Trust said before hanging up the phone.

Trust got off the bus two blocks from Boom. The heat from the police stopping almost every car with tinted windows had forced him to use public transportation. Driving around with $5 million in diamonds wasn't too much of a good idea anyway. Boom had set up a deal with his drug connect who was interested in the stones, but the only thing that really worried Trust was making this kind of deal in the hood, knowing how ugly it could get when that amount of money was at stake. That was why Trust brought two guns instead of one.

Walking up to the house, he could see a couple of guys standing outside with large guns in their hands pointed at anything that moved down that street. They must have been his connect's foot soldiers, because Boom's guys didn't dress the way they were dressed, complete with Stacy Adams gangsta hats and shoes.

Boom was standing at the entrance of the door and welcomed Trust with a thug-love hug. Trust could see a fat old man sitting at the dining room table, surrounded by a few more of the same guys who were outside. Standing on the inside porch, Trust handed Boom $2 million in diamonds wrapped in a suede handbag. That was what he owed him for helping him take Gutta from the Feds.

"Come on," Boom said, walking into the house. "Lefty, this is my man Trust I was telling you about," he said, introducing them to each other. "Now if you don't mind, I'd like to get down to business." Boom pulled out one of the diamonds from his bag and placed it on the table in front of Lefty.

Lefty took the diamond and began to examine it, putting his loupe on like he was a jeweler checking its clarity. The whole time, Trust took in the atmosphere of the room, plotting on the first person he would shoot if a gun battle kicked off. He also had an exit strategy to go with it.

Boom could see the look in Trust's eyes and couldn't help but smile at how little he'd changed since they were kids, always being a thinker first. At the same time, Boom too scanned the room, satisfied that for every soldier Lefty had, he had two to match him, and so the house was pretty much secure. A little crowded but it was secure.

"Where did you get these diamonds?" Lefty asked, breaking the silence in the room.

"Man, fuck where I got 'em from. You gonna buy them or not?" Trust shot back swiftly, not really up for too much conversation.

Nobody ever really talked to Lefty that way, so the tension in the room raised another notch. It even caught Lefty's attention. He looked up from the diamonds he was examining and gave Trust a look as if to say, "You better watch who the hell you talking to like that."

Lefty grabbed a bag of money from one of his boys and emptied the contents of it on the table, then tossed the large trash bag to the side. "Here's five million. You got five million in diamonds to trade?" Lefty asked, looking Trust in the eyes.

"This is two million right here," Boom cut in, trying to ease the tension in the room. "He might have to go and get the rest for you."

"Naw, I got it," Trust said, tossing the rest of the diamonds he had in his pocket onto the table, then standing up to check the money out. "Do I have to count this?" Trust asked Lefty in a slick way.

It was so slick that Lefty got up out of his chair and attempted to reach for his gun, just about fed up with Trust's smart mouth. His actions caused Trust to get up out of his chair and pull out twin Glock .40-calibers from his waist, pointing one at Lefty and the other at one of Lefty's guards who too pulled his pistol. Everybody in the room drew their guns, including Boom, pointing it in the direction of the guard who had his gun on Trust. The room was silent for a moment as everybody looked around at each other, willing to shoot one another.

"Ho! Ho! Ho! Everybody just chill out for a second, and let's defuse this!" Boom yelled out, still not lowering his gun so fast. "You got ya diamonds, and you got ya money. Don't turn this into a bloodbath, 'cause then nobody's gonna make it out of here to enjoy any of this shit."

The room was tense, and it took about a minute for everything Boom was saying to register in everyone's head. Lowering his pistol and chuckling, Lefty called Trust a crazy muthafucka as he bagged up the diamonds, signaling with his hands for his boys to lower their guns.

Most people would have backed down from Lefty or probably would have been killed, but not Trust. He didn't care who you were. Just as long as you could bleed just like him, everything was fair game. Lefty actually respected that in a young buck like Trust. With a final stare, Lefty left the house with his boys.

Noticing an unmarked car sitting in front of his house, Gutta went in through the back way, going unnoticed as he climbed through the basement window. Being that he was the most wanted man in the commonwealth of Pennsylvania, the two agents sitting outside his house didn't think that he would be stupid enough to come there.

While in the basement, he looked to see if anybody had been in the secret compartment he'd made in the brick wall behind the minibar. No one had. In it, he had some money, two handguns, and a burnout cell phone that couldn't be traced to him. He didn't want to take the chance of going upstairs to see what Wanda had taken, but from what Angela had told him, she'd left with everything. What he had was enough, especially since all he had to his name was the $50 Trust gave him for food.

The thought of calling Angela ran through his mind strong. He was hoping she was everything she said she was, which was loyal to him, but now wasn't a good time for that. There was more important business to take care of. Before he left the city, he wanted to free himself of the law, which meant tying up all loose ends. For now, the diamonds were in a safe place, which meant that as long as he had them, he would always have some kind of leverage.

Gutta grabbed the things he needed and left the house the same way he came in. Three blocks away he had a squada, a low-key car that he never really drove so nobody would recognize him if he rode through the city in it. When Gutta first began robbing banks, he had to prepare for times like this. One thing he'd never thought of, however, was having a chick on his side. Gutta didn't give a damn if Angela was the ugliest female he'd ever had the displeasure of knowing. As long as she was offering him a way out, he would have used her. The fact that she was gorgeous, though, that was what had Gutta feeling some type of way. He didn't want to be a sucka for a pretty face and a nice body, however, so he was trying to play it cool. Only time would tell just how serious Ms. Angela Bell was about him. If she was stringing him along in an effort to get his riches, not even God would be able to save her.

Chapter Twenty-three

Zoe walked into the grocery store and right to the back while acknowledging Ms. Mary at the register waiting on a customer. She knew exactly who Zoe was, but this was Trust's store, and she knew the relationship the two of them had, so questioning him or calling the cops on him was out of the question. In fact, throughout the summers, she grew to like Zoe. She called him Zoey.

Jarara, who shared any and all information she had with Jamita, was informed that Trust had a couple of stores in the neighborhood, so she decided to hang around to see if he would show up to check on his business. *It isn't Trust, but Zoe is good enough,* she thought, watching him enter the store. She knew it was him because his looks hadn't changed much from the pictures she had of him and the rest of the crew. She had on a pair of blue jeans, a white T-shirt, and some Nike track sneakers, blending into the city's South Philadelphia section. She came into the store, but Zoe was nowhere in sight. Pulling out her gun that was equipped with a silencer, she pointed it at Ms. Mary, who immediately grabbed the cross that was around her neck and started saying a silent prayer.

"Where is he?" she asked in her strong Russian voice.

Although Mary was kind of old, she still was from the streets. As she reached under the counter, stretching her fingers to reach for her gun without Jarara knowing what she was up to, she nodded in the direction of the back of the store, hoping she would turn to look. She did, but when she didn't see anybody, she pulled the trigger of the gun that was still pointed at Mary, striking her in the face, knocking her out of the chair she was sitting in. She fell to the ground, clutching the gun she was reaching for.

Coming out of the back room, Zoe was approaching the counter, saying some stuff to Mary, but he couldn't see her because Jarara stood in front of the counter like she was paying for something. When Zoe got close enough, Jarara spun around and pointed the gun right at his face, leaving about two inches of space between the gun and his nose.

"Where are my diamonds?" she asked, looking him in the eyes.

"I don't know what you're talking about. You got the wrong guy, lady."

That was the wrong answer. Jarara pressed forward with the gun, now touching his cheek with it. Just as she was about to pull the trigger, the front door swung open and three kids ran into the store, grabbing Jarara's attention. Zoe thought that he didn't want to die like this, and that boosted his adrenaline, forcing him to do the unthinkable when she turned to look at the kids. Zoe grabbed her arm that had the gun in it, holding on for dear life. To be a woman, Jarara was strong, putting up a fight for the gun. She was being slung around the store like a rag doll, but still would not let the gun go.

Squeezing the trigger and emptying the clip, Zoe sat on top of her schoolyard style and commenced punching her in the face, breaking her nose and covering her white T-shirt with blood. The screams from a child were all that snapped him out of his zone. He looked over to see one of the kids who'd run into the store holding his arm. He ran right over to him and picked him up. Coming out of her daze on the ground, Jarara reached for the gun that was still clutched in Ms. Mary's hand. Zoe saw her grab the gun and quickly turned around to run toward the back of the store with the kid in his arms, barely dodging the bullets hitting the soda machine and potato chip racks. Jarara struggled to get up, now determined to kill Zoe more than anything.

Zoe made it to the back room, where he left his gun, put the kid in the closet, and headed back out to the front of the store, where he was met by gunfire. Using police tactics he learned from Trust, Zoe clutched his gun with two hands, got down on one knee, reached around the deep freezer he was behind and started firing, striking Jarara in the leg, making her turn on her heels and run out of the store. He wanted to get the kid out of the store, but he didn't know if she would be waiting for him to come out, so he went through the back door, handing the kid to the first adult he saw.

Who the fuck was that bitch, and how did she know about the diamonds? Zoe thought, leaving the scene on foot. "Why da fuck this bitch tryin' to kill me? Damn, Trust, pick up your phone," he mumbled.

First Steve, the manager from the bank, and now Ralley being dead too made Angela curious as to where these diamonds came from. She had been sitting in her office all morning doing research on the diamonds, tracking down the original owner of them to see what kind of people she was dealing with. Her phone had been ringing since last night up until this morning. The Cubans wanted to know if the deal was still on. The only problem was that she only had one diamond, worth about a quarter million, which was far from what she said she could get.

"Last known place of the diamonds: Russia," she mumbled to herself, looking at the computer screen after gaining access to the bank's records. "Russia? How the hell did they get here?"

Angela sat there, digging and digging, getting all the information she could find on the owner of the diamonds. She had found out about the Kilvalshike family and how they'd become Russia's number one crime family. She called Russia to find out more information about them, but the police there seemed scared to even talk about them. She also found out about the diamonds' history and how they had belonged to a queen from Russia in the 1800s. The diamonds were actually worth more than $20 million because of their history. It was all coming together now. It was clear to Angela that there were more people after these diamonds, and they were willing to kill for them.

The death of Ralley had the whole agency up in arms, and IA was snooping around FBI headquarters, trying to get some answers. There were too many deaths of too many law enforcement officers in such a short time, which was enough for IA to stick around.

Trust brought his car to a stop just a couple of blocks from his store, where Zoe wanted to meet. Not even having to get out of the car, he could see police and ambulances everywhere. The store had yellow tape going around it, which meant somebody was killed. Trust flipped his phone out to call Zoe, and he picked up on the first ring.

"Yo, come get me!" Zoe yelled into the phone.

"Where are you?"

"I'm on Tasker Avenue, where the projects used to be. When you get to the Chinese store, beep ya horn and I'll be right out."

Trust hung up, wondering what in the hell could have happened. He was so caught up in the situation he didn't even notice the car pulling off behind him and following every turn he made.

It was Jarara. She stayed behind and sat in her car a couple blocks from the store to see if anybody she recognized would come to the scene. More specifically, Trust or Gutta. She kept a good distance from them, calling Jamita's cell phone to let her know what was going on. When Trust pulled over to the Chinese store, she pulled over too, taking the time out to check the bullet wound to her leg and change her T-shirt. Instead of jumping out of the car and having a gun battle, she sat back and waited for them to lead her to the diamonds. She was fighting the temptation of killing Zoe for tossing her around the store like a rag doll and busting her face up pretty bad. The wound was still fresh enough that she could taste the blood in her mouth, inciting the rage inside of her. She planned to take a page out of Fashkon's book and make Zoe's death a gruesome one.

Chapter Twenty-four

Gutta boldly drove into Center City like he wasn't wanted for murder at all and pulled right into the parking lot of the Season Hotel, where Angela had told him the witness would be until they found another safe house for her. He sat in the car, put the silencer on his gun, and tucked two clips into his jacket pocket. Disguising himself, he put on the full garment of a Muslim woman, with the veil that covered the face and the khimar that covered his head. It was a perfect way to go unnoticed by hotel staff, but he knew for sure Allah was not pleased with him. All about his issue, he entered the hotel and took the lobby elevator to the twentieth floor, east wing of the building. According to Angela, the witness was in room 2010, but two agents stayed three doors down in room 2016, watching her room through surveillance cameras.

Gutta walked down the hall and right up to room 2016, hoping that he was successful kicking the door in on the first try. Taking a deep breath and pressing his back to the wall, he raised his foot and kicked the door in, firing his gun coming through the door. The two agents actually turned out to be just one sitting at the monitors as bullets ripped through his body, tearing chunks of meat out of his back, killing him on the spot. Turning around to leave the room, Gutta noticed two hotel room keys lying on the bed, and he grabbed them on his way out the door.

He got to room 2010 and tried to use one of the key cards, which denied him access. Using the other card, the green light at the handle came on, popping the door open. With his gun clutched in his hand, he pushed the door open and raised his gun, entering the room with only one thing on his mind: murder.

Sitting in a chair with a gun pointed at him when Gutta entered the room was Angela. She sat there with a smile on her face.

"I knew you would come here," she said, keeping her eyes on him.

Gutta looked around the room to see if the witness was there but was brought back by the sound of Angela cocking the hammer back on her gun. It was a face-off, and the silence in the room wasn't making anything any better.

"Where is she, Bell?" Gutta said through the veil, calling her by her last name to remind her that he wasn't playing with her.

"She's not here. I couldn't stand by and let that young girl die. She's only a kid, Gutta. I will guarantee that you will never have to worry about her telling on you. I made sure of that," Angela said, lowering her gun to show Gutta she meant no harm.

Gutta wasn't trying to hear anything she was talking about. He stood still with his gun pointed at her, not even thinking about lowering it. The thought of killing her ran through his mind, but his affection had grown too strong inside of him, and he couldn't bring himself to do it. Not even when she lowered her weapon, no longer being a threat, could he bring himself to do it. But just in case she changed her mind, the gun would continue to be pointed at her.

"Are you going to shoot me?" she said, seeing he wasn't lowering his gun. She walked up closer to him, pressing her chest up against the gun like she was trying to walk through it.

The look she gave Gutta was the look of a woman who had fallen for a thug, and he could see the sincerity in her eyes. Lowering his gun, he turned around to leave out the room, when at the door stood Jamita, holding a gun in her hand down by her waist.

She wore stilettos, a miniskirt, and a jean jacket with a tank top under it. "Diamonds," was the only word she said.

This prompted Angela to react on instinct, pushing Gutta to the side as she raised her weapon, firing at Jamita, blowing holes in the wall right next to her head.

Jamita, who ran deeper into the room, shot back at Angela before diving into the bathroom. She was crazy enough to run toward the gunplay instead of running away from it. Gutta took cover behind a table he kicked over, and Angela ducked behind the bed.

"Who da fuck is dat, Angela?" Gutta yelled over to Bell, who fired a few more shots into the bathroom.

"All I want are the diamonds," a creepy voice came from the bathroom. "You give me the diamonds, and I'll let you live. If not, I will kill the both of you," she said.

Angela knew exactly who she was from the bank surveillance and from the research she did on the Kilvalshike family. She was pretty sure she had killed the bank manager and possibly Agent Ralley. Gutta didn't know what was going on, but what he did know was that whoever she was, she wasn't getting those diamonds, and it was very possible she wouldn't leave this room alive.

Popping out her clip to see how many bullets she had left, Jamita found herself being four bullets short of a ten-shot clip and outnumbered two to one. So, it was pretty much time for her to exit stage left, empty-handed but with her life.

"I'ma count to five, and if you're not out of that bathroom, you sick Russian bitch, I'm coming in!" Angela yelled from behind the bed. "One, two, three—"

Jamita came running out of the bathroom firing, making both Gutta and Angela take cover. By the time they came up to shoot, she was gone. Just like that, the woman they thought they had trapped was nowhere in sight.

Getting up from behind the table, Gutta looked outside the room window and could see a flock of police cars pulling up around the building. His first thought was that he was going back to jail. He didn't know how he was going to get out of the building without coming in contact with the cops. He started to panic, but the soothing touch of Bell grabbing his hand calmed him.

"I want you to do exactly what I tell you, and you will be all right. I have to stay here, or it will look suspicious that I walked out of the room with the person who just tried to kill a federal witness. When you leave this room, there's a service elevator at the end of the hall. It'll lead you to the kitchen area. When you get to the kitchen, go out the doors. That'll lead you to the loading dock. No cops should be back there. That's our emergency route in case we had to get our witness out of the building. There are no cameras on the service elevator, so take that stuff off before you get to the kitchen. Here's my number. Call me when you get somewhere safe, and I'll come pick you up later," she said, handing him one of her cards. "Oh, and for the cameras in the hallway, I need you to run out of the room and fire two shots back into the room so it looks like you were shooting at me."

Gutta turned to leave, but Angela grabbed him by the face, lifted the veil, and kissed him, telling him to be careful. It was a shock to Gutta, and if it weren't for her pushing him out the door then firing two shots into the wall behind him, he probably would have stayed to kiss her back.

Wasting no time, Gutta did everything she told him to do: down the service elevators and right out the back door. To Gutta, the relationship between him and Angela was official, because she just had the chance to either kill him or put him back in jail, but she let him go. It had to be deeper than the diamonds, Gutta thought, getting into the car and pulling out from the parking lot. More surprising to him was how the Russian chick found her way to the hotel and how she knew about the diamonds. With only $10 million left in diamonds to himself, they would have to stay hidden until he figured out what was going on.

Trust and Zoe walked into the hotel room where Amy was talking on the phone with one of her employees, giving him the okay to open the lounge back up.

"We gotta get out of the city tonight," Trust said, grabbing the bag of money from under the bed.

Amy ran over to Zoe and gave him a hug, happy to see that he was okay, but quickly focused back to what Trust was saying. "What's goin' on? Is everything all right?"

"Apparently we're not the only ones who want these diamonds. Some crazy chick with an accent just tried to kill Zoe, asking him about the diamonds," he said, moving around the room, pulling out money and loading up guns. "I say we just take what we got and leave. We can sell the rest of the diamonds another time."

Trust poured the money from the deal with Lefty onto the bed. "There's three million here. That's a million apiece for now. That should get us far away." He turned to look at Amy. "You can stay here if you want. The cops are not looking for you, and I don't think anybody knows you're a part of the crew. I'ma tell you this, the chick who shot at Zoe is still out there somewhere, and if she found him the first time, there's no telling who she might find next and try to kill."

"I shot da bitch, so she might be somewhere tryin' to take care of that," Zoe said, checking his gun to see how many bullets he had left in his clip.

"Well, everybody knows that I'm safe by now, and the lounge is back open today, so I'm rollin' with you, Trust. We got a few things to iron out before you think about leaving my life for good. Plus, we're a crew, and I won't sleep right until I know for sure that the both of you are somewhere safe."

Trust sat on the bed and split up the money. "We got to change hotels one more time. It's not good to stay in one spot for too long so people start noticing who we are. When we leave here, Amy, I need you to rent a car. Nothing fancy, just something that can get us out of the city. Take my car. Zoe and I will catch the bus. When you get the car, call me. Zoe and I will be at the Alpine Inn Hotel on Baltimore Pike."

Packed up, Zoe, Trust, and Amy headed for the door. It was the all-too-familiar sound of a spitball leaving the straw that caught Zoe's attention as he opened the door, taking two shots to the body, hitting him in the chest and lower abdomen. Several more bullets crashed through the window, shattering glass all over the floor. Trust grabbed Zoe and dragged his body into the room, trying to avoid being shot. Amy stood on the side of the now-broken window and could see Jarara behind a parked car. The hotel room was on the ground level, which made it easy for Amy to see her target, firing back at Jarara.

It seemed like everything was in slow motion to Trust, putting pressure on the bullet wounds that wouldn't stop bleeding. Zoe was coughing up blood and going into shock right in front of Trust's eyes. "Stay with me! Stay with me!" he yelled out at Zoe, cradling him in his arms, pulling out his cell phone to call an ambulance.

He didn't even acknowledge the bullets from Jarara's gun flying over his head, barely missing him. Amy was doing her best but couldn't get a clean shot because Jarara used the cars in the parking lot well, weaving in and out of them, getting closer and closer to the room.

Trust looked down at Zoe to see him take his last breath, dying with his eyes open. The tears couldn't stop falling from Trust's eyes as a quick flash of memories went through his head of some of the good times he and Zoe had. Amy turned in time to see Trust letting go of Zoe's lifeless body, grabbing his gun from the floor, and storming toward the door. Seeing he was on a mission, Amy stuck her gun out the window and began firing at Jarara, forcing her to get low behind a car.

It was like Trust had no fear walking out the door, looking around to see where Jarara was. Spotting her head peeking up from behind one of the car's windows, he too got low, creeping up behind her while she continued shooting at Amy, who by now had run out of ammo. She didn't even know Trust had come out of the room and was a mere two cars in front of her, waiting for the right time to strike. Jarara kept shooting into the room, walking up closer to it as she fired, emptying out a whole clip. Trust gave her no time to reload, spinning around the car and firing a single shot to her chest, knocking her to the ground. Walking up to her, he continued to fire, putting countless bullets inside her chest, neck, and face. Not done and still full of rage, Trust reloaded his gun and emptied a fresh sixteen-shot clip, all into her head. It was personalized punishment for the death of Zoe.

"We gotta get out of here!" Amy came running out of the room with the bags of money, throwing them into the back seat of Trust's car.

Trust was heading back to the room because he didn't want to leave Zoe, but Amy pulled him to the car, snapping him out of his daze. There was nothing he could do for him, and if he tried to stay with him, he was sure to go to jail, because you could actually hear sirens in the distance.

"Please, Trust, get in the car," she said. She was almost to the point of crying because he didn't want to leave. While he was getting in the car, she pulled out of the parking lot, not even giving him a chance to close the door.

Chapter Twenty-five

"We need to talk, Agent Bell," Holloway announced as he walked into the hotel room with a folder in his hand, clearing out the room so he could speak with her alone. "I got another federal agent dead. How do you explain what happened here this evening?" he said, pulling up a chair right in front of her.

"Sir, I was on watch with our federal witness against Robert Green, and out of nowhere a woman walked right through the door with a gun. I drew my weapon, trying to talk her down, and then a second woman came to the room also with a gun. I don't know what they were there for, but I identified myself as a federal agent, and that's when the shooting took place."

"Was it Gutta?"

Bell was shocked he knew his name. "No, sir. Like I said, it was two women. One of them was Muslim, and the other one I recognized from the bank surveillance when the manager was killed at First Bank."

"Well, Bell, I'ma be straight up with you. I know about the whole diamond situation, and let me be the first to tell you, I don't trust you. Hell, I don't trust anybody in that federal building. If I find out that you're not telling me something, I promise you'll be sitting in jail with the same criminals you put away. As of tonight, you're officially off the Robert Green case, and you're now on administrative leave until the conclusion of this investigation."

Angela was hot in one instant but relieved she didn't have to be on the case. She didn't even speak. She just stood up and prepared to make her exit.

"Hey, Agent Bell," Holloway said, stopping her before she left the room. "Where's the witness?"

"She ran out of the room after the gun battle, sir. I'm not sure where she is. I guess that's the job of the new agent you put on this case, to find her. If you don't mind, sir, I'd like to go home," she said, tossing her badge on the desk and leaving the room.

Holloway wasn't playing when he said he didn't trust the whole federal building in Philadelphia. That same night, a team of IA agents flooded the federal building, setting up equipment and using agents' computers, phones, and fax machines. Holloway was fed up with the amount of deaths going on in the city with law enforcement, and nobody in the federal building knew what was going on, let alone cared. Although Gutta was the primary target, his focus was on investigating every agent in the building, including the Marshals.

Faith finally answered the phone after Trust had been calling all night. She was still worried and stressing, but she was choosing to just let it go for the moment. "Hello."

There was silence on both ends of the phone for a second. "Is Erica around right now?" Trust asked, taking in a deep breath.

Fearing the worst, hearing the hurt in Trust's voice, she passed Erica the phone.

"Hey, Trust, what's up?"

Trust just couldn't find the words to say what he needed to as he cried into the phone. Words needed not to be said. Erica felt her heart beating fast and her throat starting to swell. She knew it was Zoe. His silence intensified her tears. She dropped the phone on the bed and fell to her knees, crying out for Zoe. Faith didn't even grab the phone but kneeled down next to Erica, holding her, trying her best to comfort her in this crucial time. It was a hard blow to Faith as well, knowing Zoe just as long as Trust, watching him grow up.

Amy grabbed Trust and leaned his head against her chest after he too dropped the phone on the floor, not being able to listen to Erica break down. With his birthday just two weeks away, Rodney "Zoe" Swinton had died at the age of 19, leaving behind a girlfriend and an unborn child. The streets would miss him.

Jamita stood in the morgue over the body of her dead sister. She had the doctors and staff lined up against the wall at gunpoint. She barely recognized Jarara due to the multiple bullets she had taken to the face and head at close range. After she cried a few tears, she flipped out her cell phone to call Fashkon with the news. She wrapped the body up like she was about to take it with her.

Fashkon picked up on the first ring. "Tell me who died," he answered the phone with a sixth sense of knowing when death was in the air.

"It's Jarara. I'm going to give you all the information I found out while I was in the States, and then you're going to have to send someone else to find your diamonds. I don't think I will be able to make it back to Russia," Jamita said before hanging up on Fashkon.

She couldn't care less about the diamonds now, looking at her dead sister wrapped in plastic. Then, just like the workers thought, Jamita picked her sister up and took her with her.

Chapter Twenty-six

"What's up, ma? You got a man?" Erica heard a voice call out as she rolled her eyes upward.

She was on her way to the corner store to get a breakfast sandwich from the deli. She was famished, and she didn't feel like having irrelevant conversation. Turning on her heels, she was prepared to tell off the person speaking to her until she locked eyes with him. Dude was sexy. Sexy as fuck. She wanted to hit him with a witty comeback, tell him she had a man or that she wasn't interested, but Erica couldn't find her voice.

"Cat got ya tongue, ma?" The young man before her smirked with just the slightest hint of cockiness.

Not wanting to feel thirsty, Erica came to her senses and kissed her teeth. "Not at all. Just trying to figure out if you're worth answering," she shot at him.

The guy walked toward her with the swagger of a thug and the smile of a charmer, a combination that had her panties moist off the rip. "You better believe I'm worth answering. I'm the nigga who can change ya life," he said confidently, causing her to laugh.

"Change my life? Nigga, you barely look old enough to buy alcohol. What can you do for me?" she challenged, trying not to become lost in his eyes.

Zoe waved her off. "Fuck all that. I'm that nigga, and you'll soon find out. So, you gon' answer my question, or should I just not give a fuck if you got a man?"

"If I had one, you would definitely want to give a fuck. But I'm single. And how old are you anyway?"

"I'm old enough. Believe that shit. So, let me get ya number. Maybe I can take you out on a date or something."

Erica gave Zoe a once-over. Even though he was cute, she wasn't sure she wanted to go there. She'd just started dancing a few months before, and she didn't have time to be dating, especially not a nigga who would end up having a problem with how she made her money. Erica was tired of dealing with low-level, low-budget-ass niggas. She hadn't lucked out and found a man who could provide for her, so she was going to do it for her damn self. She wanted out of the projects ASAP, and stripping was the fastest way she knew to do that. Erica didn't need an insecure, jealous-ass nigga trying to get in the way of getting to her bag.

Zoe just stared at her with all the confidence in the world, like he just knew she was going to give in, and eventually she did. She rattled off her number to him, and the rest was history.

The day they met played in Erica's mind like a movie as she cried her heart out. That damn Zoe, his ability to make her smile, was unmatched. He had a cocky yet playful demeanor that made her fall fast and hard for him. His ability to make her laugh without being an immature, goofy-type nigga made her admire him. Erica didn't know what she would do without him. She had been crying for hours. She just couldn't stop. She had been worried that he might get himself locked up, but she never expected him to go and get himself killed. Erica had begged him not to go back to Philly, but deep down she knew Zoe would never leave Trust to fight alone. Now Zoe was dead, and Trust was alive. How fair was that? Erica didn't wish death on Trust. She just wanted her man to still be living too. Why was that too much to ask?

Erica's head was pounding. Faith had cried with her and done her best to comfort her, and she'd fallen asleep. Both women were exhausted. Pregnancy was taking its toll on their bodies, and the fear they had for their men wasn't helping matters. Life would never be the same for Erica. She placed her hand on her flat belly and let out a defeated sigh. She felt so weak and so alone, but she had to go on. All she could think about now was making Zoe proud.

Gutta called Angela's phone as soon as he checked into a hotel. "Are you all right?" he asked, taking the wet clothes off from the rain that was pouring down outside.

"Yeah. I think I lost my job though, along with every other federal agent in Philadelphia. What about you? Did you have any problems getting out?"

"Naw, I made it out just fine. I need to meet with you. Can you come to me?"

"I don't think right now is a good time. I got IA all up my ass, and I'm sure they've got someone following me. Hell, I wouldn't be surprised if they were listening to me right now. "

"Damn, that's crazy. I really need to see you. Look, go to another phone and call this number. It's a burner phone that I'm just using for the first time."

"Okay."

Angela quickly pulled over and stopped at a gas station. She now regretted leaving her badge behind. It would have made some strangers less apprehensive about her asking to use their phone. Still, Angela was pretty and professional looking. If she asked the right person, they'd hand their phone over without hesitation. She wanted to see Gutta too, but she didn't want to risk being caught by anybody from Internal Affairs. Just as she suspected, the first nerdy-looking guy she asked allowed her to use his phone. When she called Gutta, he answered the phone on the first ring.

"Listen, I'm in the Red Roof Inn on Roosevelt Boulevard. I'm on the upstairs level, room 225. As soon as you get a chance, come by. I'll be here for a night or two."

"Well, let me check something out, and if I can make it, I'll be there sometime tonight. If not tonight, I will definitely be there tomorrow," she said, then hung up the phone.

Right after he got off the phone with Angela, he called Trust's phone. Amy picked up because Trust had cried himself to sleep. She told him everything that happened with Zoe at the motel. Gutta was hurt about the death of Zoe just like everyone else who knew him. Gutta never cried a tear for anyone, but as he sat on the phone listening to Amy, he cried, hoping and wishing he could have been there to take the bullet himself. Despite their differences, Gutta and Trust shared the same love for Zoe.

"You ready for this?" Faith glanced over at Erica as she drove. A few days had gone by, and everything was pretty quiet in the City of Brotherly Love, but today was also Zoe's funeral. Though neither Erica nor Faith had done anything wrong, Faith's nerves were on a hundred as she drove back to Philly. They wouldn't dare miss Zoe's funeral, but Faith was nervous about what may await them. Not to mention she was constantly worried that Trust would meet the same fate as Zoe did, and that was enough to make her physically sick. With all the stress she was under, Faith felt it would be a miracle if she didn't miscarry.

Erica sucked in a sharp breath, and then a sad smile crossed her face. "No. Not at all. This life inside of me has kept me from going insane. It's hard, Faith." Erica turned to look at her newfound friend, and she possessed the saddest eyes that Faith had ever seen. It was heartbreaking. "It's the hardest thing that I've ever been through, but I'm going to stay strong so I can always be a good mother to the one piece of Zoe that I have left."

Faith nodded as she choked back tears. Erica's strength was on a level that Faith didn't ever think she could mirror. All she could do was hope and pray that she would never have to be that strong. Trust needed to keep his word. He got them in this mess, and he needed to get them out.

Faith gripped the steering wheel. "Did you know?" she asked in a small voice. "That they were robbing banks?"

Erica sighed. "No. I honestly thought Zoe just sold drugs. When he would come home with those large amounts of cash, I just . . ." She stared sadly out of the window. "I just thought he was out hustling. I didn't even ask questions," she mumbled. "Silly of me, right?"

Faith couldn't even be relieved that she wasn't the only naive girlfriend. She never would have imagined this scenario in her wildest dreams, and it was all because she'd trusted her man enough not to question him.

During the wee hours of the morning, Trust slid through the back door of the church, avoiding the cops who were surely waiting in front of the building for people to come in. The large donation given to the church gave Trust the exclusive and discrete invitation to help prepare the body for the viewing, which only consisted of three people: Trust, the priest, and Zoe's aunt, who washed the body.

Zoe was dressed in his favorite clothes: a pair of light blue Balmain jeans, a pair of white-on-white low-top Air

Force One sneakers, a fresh white T-shirt, his iced-out chain, and a fresh haircut. He looked like he was enjoying a regular day on the block, and seeing him lying in a custom-made see-through casket took away the hurt seeing him in a wooden box would have caused. He looked like he'd just fallen asleep on a couch.

The priest gave Trust a whole hour to view the body before he started letting the public in. During that hour, Trust sat and talked to Zoe about some of the good times they had together. He cried for a while and then made a prayer for him, asking God to forgive him his sins and let him into heaven. It was a thug prayer, but sometimes God answered the thugs too.

"I'm going to start letting the people in," the priest announced, coming over to Trust, tapping him on the shoulder. "He's in God's hands now," the priest assured Trust, saying a short prayer himself.

Then Trust felt the presence of someone else behind him that almost made him reach for his gun until he saw that it was Gutta, who also slid through the back door, avoiding the law. They both just sat for the last few minutes, staring at Zoe, sharing a conversation without the sound of words.

The crowd began to roll in, so Trust and Gutta took their place upstairs in a small section of the church where they could see everybody, but no one could see them. The people didn't even notice the smell of the weed Gutta had lit up. The first to come through the doors were Erica and Faith. They drove back to the city for the funeral a couple days ago, not missing it for the world. The Feds still didn't know who Erica was, because all they had seen from that shoot-out was the nose of an AK-47 sticking out the window. They never got a chance to see her. It didn't really matter, because she was going to be there even if they did know who she was. She and Faith approached the body, already crying before they got there.

"Please wake up. Please wake up," Erica begged, crying her eyes out, kneeling in front of the casket. She stood there for a while being held by Faith, who had become her best friend over the weeks. It was her every intention to be strong, but seeing him like that did something to her. It made her knees weak, and it took everything in her not to throw up. Erica was hurting something terrible.

The people behind her understood how she felt, knowing she was Zoe's girl. As she was helped to the pews, more people came right behind her, showing their love for Zoe. The streets responded. There were so many people you would have thought he was famous, but to the people who came, he was. It was like the whole of South Philly showed up on this day.

Amy came through strong as ever, not dropping one tear. It wasn't that she didn't love Zoe, because she did. It was just the kind of person she was, which was a good thing. She showed her love by putting a green handkerchief in his casket, symbolizing the love of the crew. Afterward, she sat right behind Faith and Erica, not for any other reason but a coincidence. She overheard Erica cry out Faith's name, and she put a face to the woman Trust was so in love with. Amy thought that she was cute and could see why Trust was with her. She thought about saying something to her but didn't because that wasn't the reason she was there.

Angela showed up dressed as a civilian, showing her respect to a person she didn't even know, but she was determined to support Gutta. The relationship between the two had grown in a short time, and even though they hadn't had sex yet, they could be considered a couple. They both had some issues they needed to work out in their lives before they could commit to one another officially. In Gutta's eyes, Angela had turned out to be more than trustworthy and, so far, loyal.

Gutta and Trust sat up in the small room, looking down at all the people who entered the church. "Man, we got to talk," Gutta said, passing the blunt to Trust.

Trust didn't even smoke, but he took the blunt anyway, inhaling the smoke, looking out the small window at the crowd. "I see dat Fed bitch downstairs tryin' to blend in with the crowd."

"Yeah, that's kind of what I wanted to talk to you about. Shorty been riding out for me. I tucked her under my wing."

Trust looked at him like he was crazy. "You did what? Nigga, you must be nuts. She's a Fed."

"I'm trying to set up a meeting. She got some valuable info we could all use."

They sat there and discussed a lot of things concerning the diamonds, Jamita, Jarara, and some of the information Angela had about the diamonds. Looking down at the people, Trust choked on the weed when he noticed Amy sitting right behind Faith.

"Dog, I think it's time we get up out of here," Gutta went on. "You got ten million, and Angela and I have ten million."

"Who the hell is Angela?" Trust asked, looking confused.

"Angela is the Fed. She said she can get us a safe flight to wherever we want to go, but it can only be one-way. Once we leave, we can't come back."

"So what, you're going to fly around with ten million dollars' worth of diamonds? Then what?"

"Man, Angela set a deal to sell the diamonds to some Cuban dude she knows. That's why I need you and Amy to come to the table with us. If you want, you can just take ya diamonds and go your own way."

Trust thought about it. He did need the money for a couple different reasons, and he just wanted to get rid of the diamonds that had become more of a problem than they were worth. They were the same diamonds that had his friend lying in a casket. "Just give me a time and date," Trust said, turning his attention back to the funeral.

Jamita was on the other side of town where she dug a grave by hand in a secluded part of Fairmount Park to bury her sister. The only thought on her mind was to kill. The diamonds didn't matter to her anymore, because she'd lost the only family member she had left to an American thug. Fashkon had been trying to call her for the past few days, but Jamita refused to answer, struggling emotionally about her loss.

Jarara was buried in the clothes she died in, her face wrapped in cloth covering the many holes it sustained from the shootout. Her legacy was in Russia. Being in high ranks with the Kilvalshike family, she became an assassin and the well-respected sister of Jamita, another major link in the crime family. Her death touched many people back home, but due to the lengthy process of getting her body flown back to Russia, she would have to make her final resting place here in the United States.

Chapter Twenty-seven

There was a large memorial for the federal agents who had died over the past couple of weeks, complete with the whole 21-gun salute. Police officers from all around came to pay their respects, including law enforcement from other states. Never in the history of Pennsylvania had this many federal agents died in this short a period of time, and now not only did IA want answers, but the citizens did too.

"There's too much killing going on in the streets of Philadelphia," the police commissioner said from the podium, giving his speech at the memorial. "Enough is enough. For the men and women out there who have no regard for human life and have no respect for the lives of the police who are here to protect, we will find you, and we will hold you accountable to the highest extent of the law," he said, looking into the television cameras.

For the rest of the memorial, different people spoke about different things, including all the accomplishments the agents had, along with stories and a few jokes. It was true that a lot of people were hurting this day. A lot of tears were shed, and a lot of hearts were broken, but the taste of revenge was on everybody's mind, which made things worse.

Angela walked into the hotel room just in time to catch Gutta walking out of the bathroom with only a towel wrapped around his waist. He was just getting out of the shower. She couldn't help but notice his ripped body still kind of wet from the shower. It had been quite a while since Angela had had sex, and up until now her career, along with the small choice of men the city had to offer, was to blame for it. She had been putting Gutta off for the past week because her period came on, dick-blocking at an all-time high. Today was different. Her period had been off for two days now, but she still wasn't sure if she was ready to go that far with Gutta yet.

Gutta couldn't figure out why she hadn't given in yet, and he was starting to have mixed feelings. Did she really like him, or was it all about the diamonds? They kissed a few times and soft ground with the clothes on, but every time he went to take off her clothes, she would say, "I'm not ready yet."

"You better put some clothes on, boy," Angela said, putting the food on the table that she'd picked up for their lunch.

"Why, you scared of me? We both grown."

Not really trying to pay attention to what he was saying, she tried to change the topic to something less sexual. "You better get ready. Trust and Amy should be here in a couple of hours."

"I'm starting to think that you are bullshitting me. You're playing little games like you feelin' me, but every time I get close to you, you turn me down. What's up with dat? What? You're scared to be turned out by a thug?"

"Turned out? Nigga, you ain't ready for me yet. I'm tryin' to save ya little manhood from being hurt."

"Little?" Gutta had enough of the games. It was time for show and tell. He unwrapped his towel, letting it drop to the floor, baring his full nakedness. His dick wasn't even hard, and it hung long and low like an elephant trunk, causing Angela to swallow her last words. "There ain't shit little about my manhood," he said, walking up to her and standing next to the table.

Angela was impressed by his body, watching him walk over to her, ass naked. She couldn't say the words she wanted to say, like no.

"Stop, I'm not ready," she said as he walked up to her and put his arms around her waist.

"I promise I won't hurt you," he whispered into her ear in a soft, sensual voice that was seductive to the ears. "You gotta trust me."

Gutta took off her jacket, kissed her soft, full lips, and swiped his tongue gently across her bottom lip. Her shirt was next, and he lifted it over her head while keeping eye contact. Angela could not refuse any longer. Her body wouldn't let her. She felt sensations down below and her nipples busting through the bra. She just let herself go as Gutta picked her up and carried her to the bed, sucking on her bottom lip, and laying her down gently onto the bed. She removed her bra while he removed her pants, and her not wearing panties today was a plus. By now, Gutta was hard as a rock. He went down on her, giving her pleasure she had forgotten about, reminding her of how good it felt.

Gutta wasn't really up for too much foreplay, nor was he trying to make love. All he could think about as he looked at her thick thighs and big titties was fucking.

Coming up from eating her pussy, he wasted no time stuffing his dick inside her, making her gasp for air as he broke through the plains of her womb, digging deep within it, causing her to grab on to his back, getting ready for the ride. Her pussy was tight like a virgin but wet like the Nile River, and for a second, Gutta had to stop himself from cummin' too fast.

He played no games with her, cocking her legs back to her head and long stroking her juice box like a porn star. He was stroking at a fast pace, knocking her walls out of place. *This is what Fed pussy feels like,* he thought, going deeper inside of her like he was digging for buried treasure.

It hurt Angela in the beginning, but it quickly turned into pleasure as she came all over his dick. He could feel it gush out of her like she was pissing on him.

"Dis daddy pussy now, you hear me?" he said, letting her legs go and putting her into doggie-style position. "Let me hear you say it. Who pussy is this?"

"It's yours, daddy," Angela said, looking back at Gutta while he was punishing her from the back. "It's yours, daddy. Go deeper," she said, throwing it back at him. Her butt cheeks clapped up against his stomach, and as she felt him deep inside her, she had to look back at him to see what was making her feel so good.

Gutta fucked Angela for two hours, putting her in every position he could think of: from the front, the back, from the side, one leg up, both legs down, she got on top and rode him forward, backward, and cowgirl style. Every time he wanted to cum, he did it inside of her, unwilling and unable to pull out because of the class A goodness between her legs. It was hot, passionate, and everything each of them expected, and more.

Faith hadn't called or spoken to Trust since she'd been back in the city, so it was a sight to his eyes to see that she was calling his phone. "How are you?" he answered, trying not to sound too excited.

"I'm good, what about you?"

"I'm all right now. You still mad at me?"

"No, I'm not mad at you, but I need you to come home. I'm at the spot," she said in a low voice, referring to the house she met him at after he ran off from the police busting up in their condo.

Trust could hear a change in her tone, and it started to sound like she was about to cry. "What's wrong?" he asked, becoming suspicious.

"Somebody's here and I'm scared. Please come here," she pleaded before hanging up the phone.

Trust got up and ran out of the hotel room half-dressed and clutching his gun, leaving Amy asleep in bed. His heart was racing. He feared the worst and wanted to get to Faith as quickly as possible. Jumping into Amy's car, he peeled off into traffic.

Who the hell was in my house, and what the fuck do they want? Trust thought, driving down the highway with rage-filled eyes. He thought it may be a burglar or maybe even the cops, but whoever it was, they were surely facing death fucking around with his fiancée.

When he pulled into the driveway of the house, he checked his surroundings to see if anything was out of whack, but everything looked normal. Instead of coming in through the front door, Trust went in through the back door. Not sure what he was walking into, Trust crept quietly through the house, peeking into every room. The master bedroom door was closed. Opening the door slightly, he could see Faith sitting on the floor with a tear-streaked face and a gun pointed at her head. Holding the gun was that Russian bitch.

"Put your weapon down," Jamita barked.

Gutta had told them there were two of them. Trust didn't want to lose his cool in front of his lady, but he felt like he was walking into a death trap. He apologized to Faith with his eyes.

"What? You want the diamonds too?" Trust asked, willing to do or give anything to get her to free Faith.

"No. I just wanted to look into your eyes before I killed you," she said, firing the first shot at Trust's chest but only striking him in the left arm.

The bullet spun Trust around, knocking him to the ground. The shot was muffled by a silencer. "Noooooooo," Faith cried as Jamita got up and walked over to Trust, pointing the gun at his head.

"Wait, wait. I got the diamonds. I can give you the diamonds. Just don't shoot."

Jamita leaned in closer with the gun pressed against his cheek. She thought about killing him but stopped at the thought of getting Fashkon's diamonds. It didn't matter what happened. In her mind, she was going to kill anybody who had something to do with Jarara's death. Getting the diamonds was a plus. "Where are they?"

"I got them. They're stashed away. I'll give them to you if you just leave us alone."

"Give them to me!" she demanded, now walking over to Faith and putting the gun to her head.

"I have to go get them. Please don't hurt her," Trust pleaded, holding his arm. "I promise I'll get them to you. Just give me a time and a place."

"Go. Bring the diamonds back here. I will wait for you with your pretty little girlfriend," she said, poking the gun against Faith's head.

"What? I look stupid? The second I bring those diamonds back here, you'll kill the both of us. Let her go first. She doesn't have anything to do with it."

As badly as Jamita wanted to kill Trust, she thought about the reward from Fashkon if she could bring the diamonds back and also how easy it could be to find Trust and kill him later. She could let them go anytime she wanted and tail them and watch their every move until she felt like striking again.

"You think you're smarter than me, American boy? There's nowhere you can hide from me. No matter where you go, I'll be watching you. Have my diamonds by tomorrow morning. I will call you and tell you where to meet me," Jamita said, picking up Trust's gun and walking out the door.

He quickly ran over to Faith still sitting on the floor in shock crying and not wanting to be touched by Trust. This was the reason Trust had wanted her out of the city, but she was hardheaded and came back. He wanted to tell her this, but for now, getting her somewhere safe and as far away from the city as possible was the immediate plan. She didn't even think about the fact that Trust had been shot. The blood leaking from his arm didn't even alarm her. Faith just wanted to know why her life had suddenly been turned upside down. Her entire world had been changed in one day.

"What is going on, Trust?" she cried out. "What did you do to these people?"

"Nothing, baby. Come on, we gotta get out of here now," he said, picking her up to her feet and getting her out the door. "I'm sorry. I'm sorry," was all he could say.

Behind his concern for the safety of her and the baby, Trust was hot. *This crazy Russian bitch was just about to kill me and my girl,* he thought, putting Faith into the car. "You got to leave. You can't stay here."

"Where am I going to go? She knows about me being in Florida. She wrote down my name and my social security number," she said, finally paying some attention to the bullet wound. "She knows everything."

"Look, I'ma take you to the airport, and whatever airplane is leaving next, you get on it. Don't even tell me where you're at until I finish this business here. That crazy bitch won't be alive long enough to find out where you are anyway. Look at me. Look at me," he said, catching her eye while driving. "I love you. I promise this will all be over soon."

"What about Erica? She's pregnant with Zoe's baby!"

"She's what? Why didn't anybody say anything? Call her and tell her we're on our way to get her. Tell her not to pack anything, just be waiting at the door."

On the way to pick up Erica, Trust made a quick stop by the hospital so Faith could grab the things she needed to patch his arm up. The meeting with Gutta would have to be put on hold for a couple hours until he could get the girls out of the city, and this time for good. There was a lot of pressure on Trust, and if he wasn't wanted and could get on that plane without being arrested, he surely would have left with Faith.

Chapter Twenty-eight

Amy sat in the lounge cleaning up the place, getting ready for the nighttime festivities. A couple of customers were there finishing up lunch before heading back to their jobs to finish up the rest of the day. Amy noticed a customer she'd never seen before. She was sitting at the bar downing shots of whiskey, not saying a word as she stared at herself in the mirror that was behind the bar. The strange thing was that there wasn't anybody behind the bar to serve her, so the only way she could have had the whole bottle of whiskey was if she'd reached behind the bar and grabbed it herself.

Amy went and stood behind the bar, wiping a few glasses off and watching the last of the customers leave. The waitress who was working that shift was cleaning off the tables, carrying dishes to the back to be washed. The place was empty, and the only thing that stopped it from being totally silent was the sound of the television that Jamita looked up at from time to time.

"Can I get you anything else, sweetie?" Amy asked, reaching for the bottle of whiskey, but she was yanked back when Jamita snatched it from the bar.

"You can get me my diamonds," Jamita said, looking at Amy with the evil eye, downing another shot.

The sound of the Russian accent sent a chill down Amy's spine. She knew what it was this woman had come for and how ugly it was about to get in the lounge. Amy looked down under the counter to see how far away her pistol was, hoping it was at least in arm's reach. It was. Jamita noticed her looking down and quickly checked her.

"By the time you reach for that gun, I will have already killed you," she told Amy, pushing the empty shot glass across the bar and twirling a butterfly knife in her hand.

"I don't know anything about any diamonds, lady, so I think you should leave before I call the cops."

"What about my sister? Do you know who killed her, or was that you and your little American boyfriend, Trust?"

Amy knew where this conversation was headed and that it was enough with the small talk, seeing Jamita only brought a knife to a gunfight. Amy reached for the gun, which was a bad idea because Jamita was waiting for it, jumping up from her chair, flipping the knife open. Before Amy got her fingers on the gun, Jamita had reached over and stabbed her in the neck twice, right in the jugular. Amy fell backward into the shelves that held the alcohol, knocking bottles to the ground as she grabbed her neck, hoping to stop the bleeding. The blood squirted out of her neck all over the place while Jamita just sat on the stool at the bar watching her die, pouring herself another shot of whiskey.

Amy fell to the floor but was able to grab the gun she was reaching for and fired a few shots at Jamita as her life faded away. The bullets didn't come close to Jamita, but they did get the attention of Lisa, the waitress in the back cleaning dishes. She came out from the back to see Amy on the floor behind the bar in a pool of blood and the bar totally empty. Jamita had walked out, taking the bottle of whiskey with her and leaving her knife stuck into the bar.

Lisa tried to tie a cloth around Amy's neck to stop the bleeding, but it was far too late. She died within a couple of minutes of the initial blow. This was the only recorded knife victory in a gunfight to date.

Trust had dropped Faith and Erica off at the airport and was headed to the lounge to pick up Amy so they could go to the meeting with Gutta and Bell. The traffic was backed up, and he couldn't even get to the street the lounge was on because it was blocked off. He couldn't afford to get out of the car because there were police everywhere, interviewing people by the lounge.

Trust pulled out his phone, ready to call her, but he froze at the sight of the cops bringing somebody out of the lounge in a body bag. His gut feeling told him that it was Amy and that crazy Russian bitch had something to do with it. The waitress pretty much confirmed his feeling of it being Amy, hearing her yell out Amy's name as they took the body away.

Trust put his head on the steering wheel, mentally hurt that he got Amy involved. To him it was like her death was his fault. All she'd ever wanted to do was love him, and in return, she wanted Trust to love her back. He sat there for a minute, sorting out a lot of mixed feelings he had about her, but he ultimately came to the conclusion that he did still love her despite the love he had for Faith. This was the last blow he could take from Jamita and her Russian family. *Now it's about payback, so fuck the diamonds,* he thought, pulling off.

After driving around for a while, Trust pulled up to the hotel where Gutta was, circling the parking lot a couple times to see if anybody was watching the room that was on ground level. As soon as he walked into the room, he could smell sex in the air, even though everybody was fully dressed.

"Damn, dog, you running late. Where's Amy?" Gutta asked, looking out the door before locking it, seeing if anybody was following Trust.

"Amy's dead. We got a bigger problem to deal with before we make the deal with the diamonds. This Russian bitch gotta go."

Trust began to explain what had happened at the house and how he felt she was responsible for Amy's death. You could see the hurt and frustration in his face while he was talking, going in and out of dazes and thinking about Amy. The news of Amy's death was a shock to Gutta too, and he couldn't believe what was coming out of Trust's mouth. *First Zoe, and now Amy.* Shit was wicked.

"Well, part of the reason you're here is so that I can tell you about the research I did on the diamonds," Angela went on. "They belong to a man named Fashkon Kilvalshike, a well-known and very wealthy man in Russia. He hid the diamonds in the U.S. from the Russian government, who wanted them for themselves. I'm guessing the two Russian chicks were sent to get the diamonds after Fashkon found out they were stolen."

"So how the fuck did he know we got the diamonds?" Gutta asked.

"Obviously, the people he sent over here knew how to connect the dots. Hell, how do you think I pieced together the puzzle about you guys? You left a long trail of bodies to follow," Angela said. "Look, the best thing to do is get rid of these diamonds as fast as possible, pick a destination and fly to it, never to return to the United States again. We should all have enough money to start a new life somewhere else," she said, looking at Gutta.

"All that's fine and dandy, but we can't do anything until we kill this chick. She got my girl's personal information, and I know for sure she knows about y'all, too. We got to deal with her now, or she's going to keep coming until she kills all of us," Trust explained.

Gutta chimed in, "Da bitch is probably watchin' us right now."

"So, what should we do? I got a pre-deal with the Cubans tonight. They want to see some of the merchandise before we do the real deal. I told them we would meet them," Angela told Trust.

Trust sat down in the chair, getting his thoughts together as to how he was going to deal with the situation. His main priority was to kill Jamita, but he also wanted to come out of this with a good piece of money for all his troubles and losses. Angela and Gutta weren't taking Jamita seriously and only wanted to get the money and leave the country without cleaning up the mess they would leave behind.

"All right, you go do your deal with the Cubans," he told Angela. "Take one stone with you. They should be able to know if they want to deal from that. You think you can handle that on your own?" he asked her.

"Yeah, I can handle it. Why?"

"Gutta, you're rollin' with me tonight. I got a plan on how to bring this Russian bitch out from the dark. When I leave this room, wait for me to call you. When I do, I want you to drive out to the cemetery over Southwest and wait for me. Call me when you get there. Angela, you call me after your meeting. Everybody stay on point. If you see the chick, don't hesitate to shoot her, because she's surely going to shoot you if she gets the chance."

"You know I love you. You know I do, but I have to tell you something," Trust stated as he peered into Amy's angelic face.

He was rough around the edges. He was everything that she wasn't, and their being together was causing too many problems. Until Amy had more of her own and got out from under her parents' thumbs, until Trust was financially able to support her, he had to let her go. It was the right thing to do. Her parents were right. He was a bad influence. They were making her choose, and Trust knew without a doubt that Amy would choose him every time. He loved her too much to let her do that. Way too much. He had to be a man about this and walk away from her . . . for the moment.

"Yes, I know that." *Amy's eyes searched his face for a clue as to why he was saying those words while sounding so solemn.* "Trust, what's wrong?"

"Your parents are right. You're too invested in me. You never used to smoke, and now you go in the house smelling like the finest kush. You always want to be with me. You make everything about me, and I love that. But maybe you should focus on yourself for a while." *It broke Trust's heart to see Amy's face crumble with disappointment.*

"Why are you saying these things? I don't care what my parents say. I want to be with you." *Her bottom lip quivered.*

Trust let out a sigh and pressed his forehead against hers. "Just let me get my shit together. I swear, when I come back for you, your parents won't be able to say shit. They'll see that I'm not all bad for you."

Amy erupted into tears before turning to walk away, and Trust hated every moment of it. He was only trying to make her life better, but he'd unintentionally shattered her world. But still, even after that, she remained his ride or die with no questions asked.

Trust gripped the steering wheel angrily as he drove. It was his fault. He should have walked away from her that day and never looked back. He never should have had her robbing banks with him. He brought her in on the job, and it was the reason she was dead. Trust hated himself, and he knew he would never get over Amy's death.

Chapter Twenty-nine

Angela pulled in front of the club where she was supposed to meet with Hector, a Cuban drug dealer she used to live next door to when she was growing up in North Philadelphia, also known as the Badlands. He watched Angela grow up and looked out for her family when things got tight with money. In return, Angela looked out for him when she became a Fed. She would let him know when one of his spots was about to be raided and when the Feds were trying to build a case against him. She let him know when to lie low. The relationship between them remained the same through the years, and if Angela ever needed something or some information, he would give it to her, no questions asked.

She walked into the club and saw Hector sitting in VIP with a couple of his boys, drinking champagne and making business deals over the phone. You could tell that his boys were strapped because they didn't do any dancing or drinking, and you could see the bulge on their hips that wasn't the size of a cell phone, but rather a gun.

"Hey, Ma Ma," Hector greeted Angela as she walked into the VIP section. "How's the family?"

"Hey, Hec. I see you're doin' it big like always. How's Saundra?" she asked, speaking about his wife.

"Good, good. I want to thank you for last month. If it weren't for you, I'd probably be in jail right now wasting my money on lawyers." Hector was talking about the heads-up she had given him on the informant he almost sold drugs to who was working for the Feds. "Come. Sit down," he said, patting the seat beside him. "You thirsty? You want something to drink?"

"Naw, Hec, I'm good. I just want to show you what I was talking about. Is it safe in here?" she asked, looking around for any eyes that might be looking at him.

"We're safe, Ma Ma. Show me what you got."

Angela pulled the rock from her pocket and passed it to Hector under the table. He couldn't believe the size of the diamond, and then waved for one of his boys to close the curtains so they could have a little privacy in the room.

"Damn, Ma Ma, dis a big-ass stone," he said, pulling his appraisal equipment out from his little black bag. It took him some time to run a few tests on it, but by the time he was done, he had to wipe sweat from his head. He had never seen anything like it.

"How much you got?" he asked, seeing dollar signs behind this very large investment.

"I got fifteen million worth. It was twenty, but we ran into a small problem. I can have them ready for you in two days if you like."

Hector sat back in his chair. "I do not have fifteen million. I wish I did, but Saundra would kill me if I spent that much money." He rubbed the top of his head, thinking of another price. "I can give you ten million in cash for ten million in diamonds. That's the best I can do. Plus, we can work something out with the flight arrangements we talked about."

$10 million sounded better than no million, Angela thought. It was a deal, and the rest of the diamonds would have to wait until another buyer could be found, which wouldn't be hard considering the true beauty of the diamonds. Hector was also including a one-way flight for each of them on his private jet to go wherever they wanted to go, in or out of the country. That was a deal

Angela couldn't pass up, and now all she had to do was get the diamonds from Gutta, who still hadn't gone to get them from where he'd stashed them. No matter what she did, Angela knew that Gutta didn't fully trust anybody.

Angela went to reach for the diamond from Hector. "Wait, you think I could show this to Saundra?" he said jokingly. "It might make her spend the extra five million," he laughed.

"Go ahead, you hold on to that one. Send my hellos to the misses for me," she said, getting up and leaving without the rock. She knew he wasn't going anywhere and that his money was long enough to pay for it if something were to happen to it. In fact, that one plus a lot more would be his in a couple days. What he said about Saundra was true. She loved diamonds, and if she saw that rock, it just might make her spend an extra five million just to have some for herself. *Diamonds are a girl's best friend.*

Gutta pulled up and parked by the cemetery just like Trust told him to, holding a pair of binoculars and checking the area. Gutta went to the center of the cemetery and called Trust.

"Yo, you there?" Trust answered the phone.

"Yeah, what's good?"

"All right, in about five minutes, I'ma come through the parkway side of the cemetery. Keep ya eyes open for any car that follows the route I take. She's following me, but in what car, I don't know. I'ma spin around the bin, then go up the ramp and come down Regent Street and park at the end of the block. I know a Muslim chick on that block, so I'ma step into her house for a second. Look to see if any car has followed me that far. Call me when I get in shorty's crib. Can you see the area good from where you're at?"

"Yeah, I can see everything good, dog."

"All right, here I come. Get ready," Trust said, hanging up the phone and turning on to the parkway.

The sun was going down, but it was still light outside, enough so that Gutta wouldn't mix up cars as they came down the parkway. Gutta could see Trust coming down the parkway at a cruising speed with a couple of cars behind him. They weren't close enough to see the drivers yet, but some cars were peeling off, going down different streets that broke off from the parkway. As he came around the bin, Gutta still didn't notice any suspicious cars following him because the traffic was kind of heavy, but he kept his eyes on a blue Buick with tinted windows about five cars behind Trust. It came onto the parkway behind him but was slowed down by traffic, putting a little distance between them.

Up the ramp and around to Regent Street Trust went, but Gutta still didn't notice anything. The car he had his eyes on disappeared into the flow of traffic, losing Gutta and also making him take his eyes off Trust for a moment. He caught back up to him right before he came down Regent. It was a no-go. Nobody was following Trust, Gutta thought, watching him get out of the car and walk down to the Muslim chick, meeting her at the door.

"Yo, you see her?" Trust asked, answering the phone, standing on the indoor porch, looking out the window.

"I don't see nobody, dog. I don't think she's following you," Gutta said, looking around with the binoculars.

"I know she's out there, dog. She gotta be. Damn! Look, I'ma go around the parkway one more time. Keep ya eyes open."

"Hold up, hold up. Don't move. Stay right where you're at," Gutta told Trust, stopping him at the door.

Gutta looked through the binoculars and couldn't believe what he was seeing. Sitting on the next street over, the blue Buick with tinted windows from the parkway sat with somebody in the driver's seat. "Dog, can you see over to the next street?" he asked Trust. "There's a blue Buick Regal sitting on the corner. I saw the same car on the parkway but lost it in the flow of traffic."

"All right, it might be her. Go around behind her, and I'll walk up from in front."

Trust waited a couple minutes for Gutta to get out of the cemetery and drive down the street she was on. Gutta jumped in his car and pulled onto the parkway, cocking his gun, putting a bullet into the chamber. He drove around the bin and up the ramp, around to Regent Street, but came down the next hundred block, parking just five cars behind the Buick.

Trust left the house and started walking up the street toward the car, faking like he was talking on his cell phone so it didn't look like he noticed the car sitting on the corner next to a small mom-and-pop store. With his head down low, he peeked at the car, looking through the front windshield to see if he could see anybody. It was Jamita, leaning back in her seat and trying not to be noticed. With one hand on the cell phone and the other clutching a .45-caliber ACP, Trust walked across the street in the direction of the car. To Jamita, it looked like he was about to go into the store, but as he put his cell phone in his pocket and pulled out his gun, she knew he was coming for her.

Jamita threw the car in drive and stepped on the gas like she was about to run Trust over. Trust fired four shots into the driver's side, hitting Jamita in the shoulder once, making her drive out of control and crash into a parked car. The driver's side door flew open, and she came out firing at Trust, side-stepping across the street and squeezing the trigger at the same time, forcing him to take cover behind a car. She dropped one clip and popped another one in, backing up the block, still shooting at Trust behind the car.

Trust jumped up from behind the car and was about to shoot at her but dipped back behind the car when he saw that she was backing right up into Gutta, who was standing on the sidewalk. She backed all the way up to about six feet from his gun, which was pointed to the back of her head. She didn't even know it was coming, and by the time she turned around, it was too late. Gutta fired a single shot, hitting her right between the eyes, killing her instantly. Her body slumped to the ground. She died with her eyes open, and even though she was dead, Gutta stood over her and fired the remainder of his clip into the back of her head, knocking brain fragments onto the pavement.

Trust ran up the street to where she was lying, turned her lifeless body over, and checked her pockets, finding Faith's information and taking her cell phone. If what Gutta did wasn't enough, Trust too emptied the rest of his clip into her face before getting into Gutta's car and leaving the scene.

Holloway walked into Inspector Goodell's office, tossing a folder onto his desk with a smile on his face. IA was still investigating the federal agents in Philadelphia along with the prosecutors, hoping to get some answers for the spike on law enforcement officer murders in the city.

"Ralley was after some diamonds," Holloway began. "Twenty million dollars' worth of diamonds were stolen from the First Bank in Center City a few weeks ago, and Ralley was the agent on the case. The bank teller was in on the robbery, and Ralley found out, turning her into a federal informant, hoping he could catch the guys who did it."

"Wait, you mean to tell me that all these recent killings are over twenty million in diamonds?" Goodell asked, looking at the file Holloway dropped on his desk.

"Yeah, and I think Bell was in on it, too. Ever since I put her on administrative leave, she can't be found anywhere, and neither can the witness she was protecting in a triple homicide with Robert 'Gutta' Green, one of the suspects in the bank robbery."

Holloway sat in Goodell's office and broke down everything. He put most of the pieces of the puzzle together but came to a dead end when Goodell asked, "Where are the diamonds?" He couldn't tell him because he didn't know, but he did get an anonymous tip that something big was about to go down. Who, what, when, where, and why weren't explained by the anonymous caller, but the man said he would call back with more information as soon as he got it.

At this point, neither the Feds nor the Commonwealth had a case on anybody from the crew, and they couldn't even find them to question them about anything. The Feds raided house after house, shook down drug dealers, and pulled over countless cars in the city, and still they couldn't come up with anything. Gutta was still on the streets, and that was a problem.

Chapter Thirty

Amy's funeral was huge. It was larger than Zoe's funeral, and the kind of people who came were mostly businesspeople, with the exception of a few lawyers, doctors, and police officers, all who had been to her strip club or eaten in the restaurant area. Her viewing was held at a major church in the Bala Cynwyd area of Philadelphia, where her wealthy parents lived and also where she spent her childhood years. It was hard for everyone to understand why anybody would do something like that to a woman who was so caring and understanding. Amy always wanted to help others, sometimes before she would help herself. She did a lot for the community she lived in, donating money to churches, homeless shelters, and cancer research centers.

What her family and friends didn't know was that she lived a secret life of crime and sometimes violence. She was like a modern-day Robin Hood who found herself so in love with a man that she would do just about anything for him, and in doing so she paid with her life.

The deal with the Cubans was set for tomorrow, and Angela couldn't figure out why Gutta hadn't gotten the diamonds yet. She was starting to think he didn't even have them and that he might be stalling for some other reason.

"You know the deal is tomorrow. When are you going to get the diamonds?" she asked Gutta, lying in bed next to him with her head on his chest.

It was like Gutta didn't hear anything she'd just said, turning the channel on the television with the remote control. It was starting to bother him that she kept asking for them, like she didn't believe he had them. All Gutta was trying to do was keep them safe until the deal was about to go down. He didn't want anything to happen to them before he got the chance to sell them. He quickly changed the topic, trying to take her mind off the diamonds.

"You know that one-way flight you're about to take? Where are you planning to go with your share of the money?"

She took her time answering that question, not wanting to say the wrong thing. "I was hoping you and I would be able to take that flight together and maybe go to Brazil or something. I always wanted to go to Brazil. I hear it's nice there," she said, looking up at him from his chest.

Brazil sounded good to Gutta, but what sounded even better was that she wanted him to go with her. That was kind of the answer he was looking for, because if she had said anything different, he would have thought she was up to something shady. He was from the streets, so he knew when a chick was trying to run game, but with Angela he thought she was keeping it real.

"Get dressed," he told Angela, getting up from the bed to put his clothes on.

"Where are we going?"

"Just get dressed and meet me in the car," he said. He went out the hotel room door.

When she got outside, he was already sitting in the car waiting for her. He didn't know where he wanted to go yet, but what he did know was that earlier Amy was laid to rest. He wanted to go real bad, but there wasn't any amount of money in the world that could make him risk being seen. The church she was being viewed in wouldn't take any amount of money to view the body before its due time unless it was direct family. Her family never liked Trust, so showing up to the funeral would have been a huge problem, something they wanted to avoid at all costs, especially today. For now, all they had were memories.

Angela jumped in the car with Gutta, hoping they were about to go and get the diamonds. It was getting kind of late, and in less than twenty-four hours they would be meeting with Hector.

Driving along, Gutta wanted to know more about how Angela felt about him, because depending on how she felt, it would determine whether he would get on that flight with her. He was feeling her, and the sex was grade A, but what was the point of all of it if he couldn't trust the loyalty she said she had to Gutta.

"Where do you see this thing going between us?" Gutta asked, looking out to the road ahead of him.

"Well, Gutta, I'm not going to sit here and lie to you and say that I love you, because we just met, but what I can say honestly is that I care about you very deeply, and I hope that one day I could learn to love you. I mean, it's hard to explain."

"Is it the money why you with me?"

"Money plays a part in every relationship, and if any female tells you anything different, she's lying. But I think that, had I met you under a different set of circumstances outside of me investigating you for drug trafficking, there would have been a chance I could have ended up being ya girl. Ya little street wifey if that's what you call them," she said, smiling. "Don't get me wrong, your hunger for money is attractive to me."

She talks a good game, Gutta thought. "Look in the back seat and grab that bag for me," he told her, grabbing his gun from under the seat while her head was turned, stuffing it in his jacket before she turned back around with the bag.

"What is it?" she asked, putting the bag on her lap, looking at him for permission to open it.

When she opened the bag, she couldn't believe her eyes as she dumped some of the diamonds into her hand. It was one thing to see one stone by itself, but to see so many at one time was a totally different experience for Angela. She couldn't even find the words to say how mesmerized she was by their beauty, but the look on her face told a tale of greed, something Gutta knew all too well.

"You had these diamonds with you the whole time and didn't tell me," she said, not taking her eyes off the diamonds.

"Damn, girl, breathe! You look like you about to bust a nut," he told her, trying to bring her back to earth.

You just don't know, Angela thought, smiling at the tingling sensation between her legs. "So where are we going?" she asked, putting the diamonds back into the bag they were in but also noticing a gun in the same bag, grabbing it, and putting it on her lap.

Gutta reached into his jacket like he was rubbing his chest, but really, he was clutching the Glock .40 he got from under the seat. She now had the diamonds and a gun in her possession, and Gutta was curious as to what she would do in a situation like this. If she acted like she was going to take the diamonds by force, he would open fire through his jacket before she got the chance to put a bullet in the chamber. If she put the gun back in the bag or even on her hip like the loyal bitch she said she was, then he would know she was everything she said she was.

"I was thinkin' we could get a bite to eat. You know, spend a little time together so we can get to know each other. I know you're hungry. We been lyin' in that bed all day," Gutta said, taking the safety off his gun because Angela had yet to do something with the gun on her lap.

"You think we should be driving around like this?" she asked, taking the gun from her lap and putting it in the bag with the diamonds. "How about we grab some take-out from McDonald's or something, then go back to the room and chill until tomorrow? I don't want anything to happen between today and tomorrow," she said, leaning over and putting her hand on his thigh. "I'm just tryin' to chill out. By tomorrow evening we should be ten million dollars richer, landing in a foreign country of our choice."

Gutta looked at her, smiling in agreement with the plan she had for the rest of the night, taking his hand off the gun in his jacket. She had the opportunity to rob Gutta for the diamonds and being $10 million richer by herself, but she made a life-altering decision by staying loyal. If she hadn't, it would have cost her her life, and Gutta was more than willing to end it if he had to.

Trust was trying to call Faith all day, trying to find out where in the hell she and Erica had ended up when he dropped them off at the airport yesterday. After his back-to-back calls she finally answered the phone, hardly able to talk over the noise in the background.

"I can't really hear you, babe. Let me step outside," she said, heading for the front door, stepping out on the porch. "Yeah, I can hear you now. What's goin' on?"

"Nothing. I been trying to call you all day. Where are you?"

"I came to stay with my sister in Cali. We got here a few hours ago. It took two flights to get here. My sister was so happy to see me she started calling the whole family over. Never mind that. What's up with you? I miss you so much."

"I'm good now. I took care of that situation," he said, holding the information he got from Jamita's pocket with Faith's social security number. "I miss you too. How's the baby?"

"I'm not sure. I have got to eat something soon though. I plan on calling the ob-gyn tomorrow to set up an appointment. How do you feel about moving out here?"

"I'll move wherever you want me to," he said with a huge smile on his face.

Trust and Faith talked for a while about living in Cali and raising a family there. It really didn't matter to Trust where he went. All he wanted to do was complete the deal with the Cubans and take that one-way flight outta Philadelphia. He felt like he had been in the city far too long, and if it weren't for the diamonds, he would have left a long time ago before all the warrants came into play. Leaving now without anything would be stupid, and stupid was one thing Trust could not be.

Not more than five minutes after he hung up the phone with Faith, a phone started ringing. He picked up his phone, but it wasn't his phone that was ringing. It was the phone he took from Jamita, which was in his jacket pocket across the room. "Hello," he answered.

"If you're answering her phone, that must mean she's dead," a slow Russian voice of a man said into the phone.

"Yeah, she checked out. Who da fuck is this?"

"Do you have my diamonds?"

"Why, you plan on buyin' them back? 'Cause if not, it's pointless you calling. You sent these dumb bitches down here, and they killed two of my friends. Fuck you. These diamonds are mine now."

"You must not know who I am, Gutta, Trust, or Zoe. Oops, I'm sorry. Zoe is dead, so this must be either Trust or Gutta. This is what I'm going to do: you can either return my diamonds to me, or you can start digging your grave," Fashkon said in a calm tone.

"Well, this is Trust you're talking to, and if you want your diamonds so bad, come get them."

Fashkon didn't say another word and hung up the phone in Trust's ear. Trust didn't take the threat seriously at first until he thought about the kind of people Fashkon had riding out for him and how they would risk being killed all the way in another country if needed. Plus, if he had anybody else going as hard as the two he'd sent, Jamita and Jarara, it could get real ugly in the city for a lot of people.

I got to hurry up and get the hell out of here, Trust thought, throwing the phone up against the wall.

He wasn't trying to hear anything Fashkon was talking about. In less than twenty-four hours, he would be somewhat rich, and then Fashkon would have to find him if he wanted to kill him. With $10 million, that would be like finding a black ant on a black rock in the middle of the night.

Chapter Thirty-one

Trust, Gutta, and Angela sat in the motel room loading up their guns and getting ready for the deal. They all had two handguns apiece with bulletproof vests and extra clips. The sounds of guns cocking filled the room. Even though Angela knew Hector, Gutta and Trust didn't, and with the amount of money that was at stake, they weren't ready to take any chances with this Cuban flying off with $10 million in diamonds. Hector could only spend $10 million, so the other $5 million in diamonds Trust had. He played it smart and gave them to Faith when he dropped her off at the airport.

Gutta and Angela drove in one car, and Trust drove in another, headed for the airport in Harrisburg. The Philadelphia International Airport was too crowded and the security was too high for the transaction to happen there. So, Hector wanted it to go down at a small airport he was familiar with. Not too many planes left this runway at night, so Hector's jet was clear for takeoff all night.

Trust called Gutta's cell phone, driving behind him, only about twenty minutes from the airport. "Yo, look, I don't know these dudes, so stay on point. Make sure they don't see the diamonds until we see the money. Get in, get out, ya dig me?"

"Yeah, I feel ya, dog. Make sure you watch my back," Gutta said, looking over at Angela.

"I don't know how well you trust Angela, but keep ya eyes on her, too. She's the only one who knows who's who," Trust said before hanging up the phone, making Gutta take a double look at Angela.

The night sky was clear, and the lights from the highway lamps shone into the car as Trust could see the airport up ahead. As they pulled into the airport, Hector's jet was visible, surrounded by a few armed guards at the end of one of the runways. As they parked their cars, the three got out and made their way to the jet. Hector was standing in the door of the jet, waving for his men to stand down. Hector was also on point with a lot of firepower at his disposal. He had never been robbed in his life, and tonight wasn't about to be the first time, even if Angela was at the head of the deal. Business was business, and this was the way he dealt with business.

"Hey, Ma Ma," Hector said to Angela, getting off the plane to meet her with a hug. "You're a bit early. You must have somewhere to go," he joked. "Are these your friends?" he asked, extending his hand for a shake from Trust and Gutta.

The introductions were made, and Hector invited everyone onto the jet. It was plush on the inside, complete with a bar, televisions hanging from the ceiling, and leather couches that reclined for sleeping. On the bar, there were several money machines so that the money could be counted fast and accurately.

"So, where're the diamonds?" Hector asked, looking back and forth from Angela to Gutta.

"No disrespect, but we need to see the money first. A lot of bullshit has been going on lately, and I'm really not down for the games right now," Gutta shot back, catching the attention of Angela, who thought the deal was going to go smoothly.

Hector waved to one of his guys to go and get the money. "I don't know if Angie told you guys about me, but I'm a straight-up guy. I always do good business," he said, pointing out the window to the car that pulled up to the plane.

Out from the car came two men, who carried two large bags onto the plane. They dropped them onto the floor in front of Gutta, then stepped back, grabbing a hold of the machine guns they had strapped around their bodies. Gutta cracked open one of the bags and could see a large amount of money inside. Gutta looked at Angela, giving her the approval to give him the diamonds. She stood up, lifted her shirt, unstrapped the diamonds from around her stomach, and laid them on the table.

Hector began checking the diamonds while Trust and Gutta put the money through the money machines. Angela sat with Hector and engaged in small talk while he checked the diamonds. After about a half hour, both parties were done and were satisfied with the deal. All the money was there, and all of the diamonds were there.

"So, is everything all right?" Hector asked Gutta, finalizing the deal with his seal of approval.

"Yeah, we good," he said, stuffing the money back into the bag with a smile on his face.

That same smile quickly turned into a frown when Hector's boys raised their guns and pointed them right at Gutta and Trust, giving them the indication that if they even attempted to reach for their guns, they would be gunned down. One of the guys went over to disarm Gutta and Trust, walking right past Angela, who now had her gun out in her hand.

"What the fuck is this all about?" Gutta asked, looking at Angela for an answer. "I thought you told me he does good business."

"I do," Hector chimed in. "I always do good business, but I can't stop others if they don't want to do the same."

Gutta looked over at Angela. She had a creepy smile on her face, lookin' up at him. "It's ten million dollars. What did you expect? I can't afford to break it down among three people, baby. It just won't work."

"What about us?" Gutta asked.

"You didn't think me and you would ever work, did you? I mean, the sex was great, but trust me when I tell you I'm not the girl for you."

Trust couldn't do anything but put his head down, listening to Angela talk. He also shot a mean look at Gutta as if to say, "I told you so." He never trusted Angela, but Gutta's nose was open so much he couldn't see the game.

Angela pointed the gun at Trust and Gutta and motioned for them to get off the jet. The sound of the pilot starting the engine on the jet snapped Trust out of his daze, bringing him to the reality of what was going on.

"You sure you wanna walk down this path?" Gutta asked as his final question, heading for the door.

"Yeah," Angela said, kicking Gutta in the back, making him fall into Trust, who was already walking down the steps, and then closing the door.

Gutta looked back at the door to see Angela pointing at something behind him. When Gutta turned around, he could see about five black SUVs with flashing lights coming into the airport. Angela had tipped off IA Inspector Holloway as to where he could find the most wanted men in the city. Trust looked back and saw the same, but his reaction was a lot different from Gutta's. He got up and started running. Gutta quickly caught on and did the same. It was to no avail because the cops were everywhere.

"Freeze!" one agent yelled, wearing SWAT clothes and holding a submachine gun pointed right at the both of them. "Get down on the ground!"

They both complied, watching the jet take off down the runway while being handcuffed. This was the worst feeling in the world. On their way to jail and out of $10 million, the thoughts of Faith went through Trust's head like wildfire, thinking about her and the baby. Tears filled his eyes as he thought of the judge banging the gavel on the bench, telling him he had life in prison with no possibility of parole.

Gutta just looked at the jet taking off with his money inside of it. He actually trusted Angela, thinking that they had something together. It still wasn't registering that everything happened the way it did until he was put in the back of one of the SUVs.

"We've been looking for you, Gutta," Holloway said from the front seat, flipping through a folder with all of his information. "You know, we got a lot of questions for you, and I know you got plenty of answers if you ever want to even think about getting out of jail in this lifetime."

"Man, I don't know shit. You got the wrong guy. You talk that shit to one of those rat muthafuckin' informants you got. "

Holloway smiled. "That's how all informants start out. You think about that for the next couple of days. When you're ready to talk, I'll come see you."

"Just shut da fuck up and drive," Gutta said, blowing Holloway off.

Holloway turned around from the driver seat and punched Gutta in the mouth, knocking spit from his mouth onto the window. The punch may have looked like it hurt, but there was nothing Holloway could do to match the pain of Angela's disloyalty to him.

Trust was put into a separate SUV from Gutta, and as soon as he got in the back seat, he asked for his lawyer, avoiding any further questioning by Goodell. The request for his lawyer really put a dent into Goodell's plan of getting Trust to cooperate with the government.

20,000 feet in the air, Angela sat in a chair across from Hector, having a few drinks and talking about the good

old times. One guard sat up front with the pilot while
the other two were watching a movie in the back of the
plane, counting the money Angela gave to them as a gift
for having her back with Gutta and Trust. While Hector
talked, she couldn't help but think about Gutta and the
small amount of guilt she had turning against him. For
a moment in her life, she felt somewhat happy lying up
in the bed with Gutta, enjoying the good sex and funny
conversations she had with him. He was like a boyfriend,
and that was something Angela hadn't had in a long time.
She was quickly brought out of her daze when Hector
snapped his finger in front of her face.

"Ma Ma, you still with me?" Hector asked. "Where do
you want to go?"

Angela looked around to see where everybody was. It
was time for the rest of her plan to go into effect. She got
up and excused herself, making her way to the bathroom,
putting her hand between her legs as if she had to use
the bathroom badly. As soon as she got to the bathroom,
she reached under her vest and grabbed the silencer,
screwing it onto her gun then checking the clip to make
sure it was full.

"You can do this, you can do this," she said to herself,
looking in the mirror, tucking her gun back in her waist
and fixing her hair.

Angela came out of the bathroom and walked directly
to the back of the plane where the two guards were
sitting, watching the television. They didn't even pay
any attention to her walking up behind them, turning
around a moment too late as Angela pulled the gun
out and fired the first shot into the head of Mark, the
guard sitting on the left side of the aisle. Then she spun
around and did the same thing to Joe, who was reaching
for his gun on the floor in between his legs. Hector
didn't even hear the shot, nor could he see what was

going on because he was paying more attention to the window he was looking out of, enjoying the night sky. Angela was sure to give out nothing less than headshots, trying to avoid bringing down the jet by accident.

Angela walked back to where Hector was sitting, clutching her gun as she sat in the chair across from him. Hector could see the specks of blood on her jacket and the gun with the silencer on it as she sat down in front of him. He kept a calm face and leaned back in his chair, knowing what Angela was up to.

"So now what, you're gonna shoot me too?" Hector asked, staring out the window again.

"It's not personal, Hec. It's just business."

"Damn, Ma Ma, I pretty much raised you from when you were a little kid. I fed you, I clothed you, and I kept money in your pocket all the way up until you went to college. This is how you repay me. This is your way of sayin' thank you."

"Hec, don't make this harder than it has to be. I watched you sell more dope in the streets than anybody I know. You've killed more people in one year than I could do in a lifetime, so don't take this as a surprise. You said it yourself. You raised me."

Hector thought about what she was saying and couldn't do anything but respect the game. He only wished she would take her eyes off him for a split second so he could grab his gun from under the seat he was in and blow her head off. That wasn't the case. She kept full eye contact with Hector because she knew what he was capable of. A tear fell down her face as she stood up and pointed the gun at his head. This was one of the hardest things she had to do. Hector didn't even look her in the eyes before she killed him, turning his head to look back out the window.

"I'm sorry," she said, pulling the trigger, putting a bullet in his head, splattering his brain all over the window.

She walked up to the cockpit where the pilot and the last of the guards, Mike, were. They didn't even know what was going on, and Mike wouldn't be able to find out because Angela shot him in the back of the head before he had the chance to turn around. The sight of that scared the life out of the pilot, watching Angela remove the slumped body from the copilot chair then sit down and put the earpiece in.

Inspector Holloway walked into the room, tossing a folder full of pictures on the table Gutta was sitting at, hoping the ride back from the airport gave him enough time to think about cooperating. The photos were from a few banks the crew robbed earlier in the year, but in all of the pictures, the men wore masks.

"Bank robbery, murder, drug trafficking, obstruction of justice, and escape," Holloway ran it down. "You got a lot on ya plate."

Gutta sat there with a crazy smirk on his face, listening to what Holloway was talking about. He was right, Gutta did have a lot on his plate, but during the ride back from the airport, Gutta realized a few things he didn't think about before. His smirk became a smile then a chuckle all the way into a full laugh, confusing Holloway.

"What the hell is so funny?"

"You ain't got shit on me, stupid. Bank robbery? Who's your witness? What's your evidence? Let me tell you," Gutta taunted, making a zero with his hand. "Murder? Who did I kill? Who's your witness? Where's your proof? Oh, let me tell you," he said, sticking the zero up again. "Drug trafficking? Well, we both know what happened to that witness or, should I say, informant. I watched the news," Gutta said, cleaning up his words just in case there were recording devices in the room. "You and I both know you ain't got shit."

"What about escaping from federal custody?" Holloway shot back.

"Escape? I was kidnapped while in your custody. I'm thinking about filing a lawsuit against the government for that."

Holloway was furious with Gutta. What he was saying was very much true. The Feds didn't have any evidence or witnesses placing Gutta at the scene of any of the crimes he mentioned. The witnesses were either dead or missing, and the only thing holding him was the warrants that were issued for the escape. Holloway couldn't even find Agent Bell, who could implicate Gutta in the drug trafficking and in the murders, and because he put her on administrative leave, it was highly possible that she wouldn't help out in the case anyway. Hell, Bell probably wasn't even in the country by now. $10 million in diamonds, $10 million in cash, who would want to be stuck in the country?

Chapter Thirty-two

"Trust, we got ourselves a problem," Goodell said, coming into the room, pulling up his britches and popping his suspenders before taking a seat on the table right in front of Trust. "I know you're a pretty smart guy and you're probably not going to talk, but I thought you should know that your friend Gutta is in the other room signing his statement he gave that involves you in a shitload of crimes. He told us about Monica, the bank teller, and how you killed her, her husband, and a federal agent. He told us about all the banks you guys robbed, and he told us about how you broke him out of federal custody. He told us about the diamonds. Trust, we got you. You're going to jail for a long time or might even get the death penalty, if the government pushes for it, unless you tell us what we want to know."

Trust was already familiar with the interrogation tactics the police used, so he wasn't at all intimidated by Goodell. The only thing on his mind was calling Faith to let her know what was going on. He knew that they didn't have much evidence against him because he made sure he cleaned up behind himself. It was more entertaining to Trust to watch IA run around like a chicken with its head cut off, trying to get a confession.

"I want to see my lawyer," Trust requested, making Goodell mad.

"Your lawyer's not going to do you much good. You're going to jail with or without him."

"You know, it's funny, if you got all this evidence against me like you say you do, what do you need me to talk for? If you got me, then fine, I'll see you in trial," Trust said, making those his final words for the evening.

Later on that night, Gutta and Trust were taken across the street to the detention center, where they would sit until they could be arraigned before a federal judge. The trip from the federal building to the detention center really blew Trust's mind because they were connected to each other underground. One long tunnel beneath the street led them back and forth from jail to court, not being able to see outside.

Trust was issued his green jumpsuit and sent to a pod on the sixth floor. He had never been to jail before so the whole process was new to him, and the fact that he couldn't call Faith was irritating. His cellmate was a stand-up dude from North Philly who'd gotten caught up in a drug conspiracy with a big-time drug dealer who was well known in the city. Trust didn't even get a chance to put his things away before Steven Weatherspoon, his celly, walked in. The first thing he did before saying anything to Trust was go into his locker and pull out his legal work.

"Before we get to talking up in here, we gotta get a few things straight," Steve began. "I don't mean no disrespect, but if you are a rat, you gotta find another cell. I don't deal with no hot niggas. I don't care who you are. If you are one of those stink-butt, poop-butt, sham, moody niggas, then you got to find another cell. Ain't no faggot shit jumping off up in here. If I find out later on down the line that you were either one of those two things and you're still in this cell, we're gonna have problems," Steve said, passing Trust his paperwork.

Trust looked at Steve like he was crazy. *Who the hell does this nigga think he is?* Trust thought. Trust felt some type of way about the whole rat thing. It wasn't in his blood to tell on anybody, but as Steve continued to explain how things went in this jail, he could see why it was so important to him.

"If you were smart, you wouldn't talk to anybody about your case. There's dudes here who will jump on your case so they can testify against you for a time reduction," Steve informed Trust.

He pointed out in his paperwork where it said that he wasn't cooperating in his case. After showing him that, Steve quickly took the paperwork back from Trust and put it back in his locker. He didn't want to let Trust get a chance to see what his case was about.

"Instead of sitting back watching TV and thinking that your lawyer is going to do everything for you, you need to get in that law library and figure out a way you can win ya case and get da hell up out of here. The Feds is a whole other ballpark than the State. These people over here is wicked, and their conviction rate is through the roof because of all the niggas who's telling on each other. So, strap up and get ready for a rumble, because it's going to be a hell of a fight."

Trust couldn't sleep all night thinking about what Steve had said and the fact that he couldn't call Faith yet. It wasn't until he heard one of the Muslim brothers calling the brothers to prayer that he noticed it was 5:00 in the morning. He realized that Steve was a Muslim, too, getting up and wiping water over his face, arms, head, and feet before laying his prayer rug out. Trust knew a little bit about Islam from his cousin Rafiq, who used to tell him about it when he was younger.

When the cell doors were unlocked by the guard, Trust got out of bed just in time to catch the 6:00 news coming on. The volume on the TV was muted, and the only way you could hear the TV was with headphones, something Trust didn't have. Seeing that Trust wanted to listen to the news, Steve walked over and gave him his Walkman so he could hear. It was right on time, seeing the news reporter standing on the runway of the Harrisburg airport.

"Top story this morning," the reporter said. "Five men are dead and police officials haven't a clue as to what happened last night in this fatal shooting. Late last night, airport officials noticed this small aircraft sitting on the runway with the doors opened and the lights still on. When they boarded the plane, they discovered five dead bodies, including the pilot, shot to death. There were no signs of a struggle, and none of the bodies have been identified at this time. We'll bring you more coverage as the story unfolds," the reporter said before the news switched to another story.

Trust couldn't believe what he'd just heard. With five men dead, that must have meant Angela was alive and possibly the one who did the killings. Trust just looked at the TV and was still shocked. He was brought back to his senses when the guard yelled out his name, telling him that he had to go to court. Trust had the feeling that the Feds wanted to question him about the murders, but he also thought about having the best alibi, being that he was in jail at the time of the murders.

"Look, when you first get locked up, the Feds do interviews to see if you will cooperate on your case. Don't make it a habit going across that street," Steve told Trust as he was sitting in the cell getting ready.

Trust was pretty much fed up with Steve and his thoughts of him being weak enough to become a rat. "Check dis out, fam," Trust said, picking his head up from washing his face at the sink. "I don't know what kind of niggas you fuck with, homie, but I'm far from a rat. I find it highly offensive that you would even consider some shit like that. If you only knew the kind of caliber nigga you was in the cell with right now, you wouldn't fix ya lips to say half the shit that you saying. I'm the type of nigga you would love to have on your team, so do me a favor and cut out da bullshit rat jokes. That's all it is to me, my nigga, a joke," Trust said, standing in the middle of the cell, waiting for any repercussions of what he'd just said. "I'll holla at you when I get back from court," Trust said, seeing that Steve didn't say anything.

When Trust got downstairs to the holding cells, he saw Gutta walking past, going into the cell next to his. He quickly jumped up to the door and asked the guard if Gutta could be put in the cell with him so they could talk. The guard denied Trust's request and informed him that they had a separation put on the both of them. That meant they couldn't be around each other under any circumstances. That was an order the prosecutor put on codefendants in case one of them decided to start cooperating. The prosecutor also didn't want them to get their stories together before the agents had another chance to interview them.

Gutta came out of the holding cell to be handcuffed by the Marshals first. He was able to get off a small conversation with Trust in the process. He had to talk fast and pick his words wisely because the Marshals were moving fast.

"Did you see the news this morning?" Gutta asked, thinking about Bell.

"Yeah, I saw it. Listen, these people don't have anything on us. Lack of information means lack of evidence," Trust shot back, thinking about all the things his celly told him.

Gutta nodded his head in agreement. That was pretty much the end of the conversation. Nothing more needed to be said. This wasn't Gutta's first time in jail, and he knew how not to talk to the police and give statements. He too had been bred by a stand-up man and surrounded himself with those exact kind of people as he was growing up. Although the Feds were new to him, the same rules applied from the Commonwealth's system.

They were both taken across the street only to be interviewed by the IA agents who had locked them up. Trust and Gutta both declined to talk. It was a tough blow for the Feds because they knew that Trust and Gutta had all the answers they were looking for concerning the five dead bodies in the jet that was found this morning. They were trying their best to link Bell to this case and even offered freedom to whichever person decided to talk first.

It was to no avail. The interviews lasted every bit of twenty seconds. The agents were so mad that they called over to the jail and told them to put Trust and Gutta in the hole for a few days, another tactic they used to try to break someone. Later, they would find out that that kind of tactic didn't work on people like Gutta and Trust, but for now, it was time to be arraigned before the judge.

Chapter Thirty-three

"You okay?" Faith asked Erica as she handed her a cup of hot tea. It seemed like they asked each other that question several times a day.

Erica wasn't really okay. Neither was Faith. But they made an effort to remain strong for each other. Erica gave Faith a small smile. "Yeah. I just got off the phone with a caseworker. I have officially applied for Medicaid in California."

Erica was determined not to go too much longer without prenatal care. Being on the run from danger and her lack of money had prevented her from finding a doctor, but the women were settled in Cali. Faith had emptied her bank account, and Erica had money stashed from when Zoe was alive and taking care of her. Both women were in their first trimesters, and they weren't against getting jobs. They were now a team. They split the cost of a small two-bedroom apartment and furniture. Cali living wasn't cheap, but they decided to save the money they had left for when they gave birth.

In order to pay some bills, they knew they would have to get jobs. Erica hated the thought of stripping while pregnant, but she knew she had at least another two months before she started showing. She didn't have a college degree, but she knew the gift of gab. If she danced five nights a week for the next two months, she'd surely be able to put away enough to live off of during the remainder of her pregnancy, especially if she and Faith were splitting everything down the middle.

The women hadn't spoken to Trust, but they could only hope he would come through for them. Faith had only briefly spoken to her parents, and she was so embarrassed and ashamed of what she'd done. She didn't want to worry them and tell them that Trust feared for her life. By her fleeing the city, it made it look like she was guilty of something, but the only thing she was guilty of was loving the wrong man.

It took every trick in the book plus a few favors upstairs for the prosecution to come up with enough evidence to bring formal charges against Trust and Gutta. When they did, they threw everything but the kitchen sink at them, and there wasn't a lawyer in the city who was vicious enough to take on the Feds when they were in this type of element. It was feeding time. Armed bank robbery, murder, and escape were just a few of the charges that were going to end up on the indictment. Trust and Gutta had already lost the fight before it even started. Everything they worked so hard for was pretty much out the window. With all the mayhem they'd caused in the city during the past few weeks, it seemed like everybody in political authority was against them, even the judge who had their case.

With $20 million in diamonds still on the streets, along with about $15 million in cash, one could only imagine how sick Trust and Gutta had to be, having no way of reaching out for assistance. Sadly, they had public defenders for the time being, and there was no way in hell they would win a trial in this manner. Faith and Erica were on the other side of the map, and Trust didn't want to risk the chance of exposing them while he was in jail. Her safety always came first, and honestly speaking, there wasn't too much money could do for Trust right now.

Angela, on the other hand . . . well, you know Angela. She was probably on foreign land somewhere in the south of France.

From the outside looking in, Trust and Gutta were fried fish, but from the inside of a jail cell looking out the window, Trust knew beyond a shadow of a doubt that Fashkon was coming for his diamonds. He knew the kind of drive and ambition Fashkon had the first time he sent for the diamonds. It was only a matter of time before he was going to be coming for them again, and when he did, there were only two people in the world who knew where the diamonds could be found, and they were Trust and Gutta. The "diamond rush" wasn't over by a long shot. It could never be over. Fashkon would make sure of that, all the way up until he took his last breath. The rush continued. Diamonds last forever.

To Be Continued

Notes